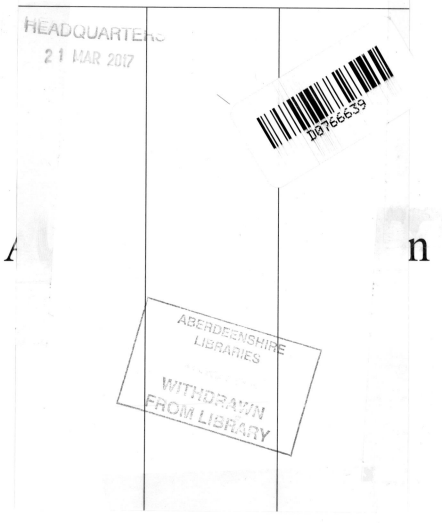

A   n

ISBN-13: 978-1480022058
ISBN-10: 1480022055

**FT
Pbk**

Cover illustration by Leslye Writer

DEDICATION

For the many friends I met in Second Life ™ and with special thanks to Leslye for
the cover illustration

CONTENTS

What others said about *Alternative Dimension*

"… for all its dystopian menace, the story is carried along by its sparkling humour and we find ourselves enjoying the fate of those seduced by the promise of virtual bliss."
—Edgar

"I liked the humor … and the sometimes absurdly comical events that take place in AD's world"
—Heikki Hietala

"… there is humour aplenty. Like a picaresque novel, or a weird modern version of *Pilgrim's Progress*, or maybe even a *Canterbury Tales* for our times"
—Cally Philips

PROLOGUE

Stitchley Green hated mirrors as much as he hated his name. His parents, Samuel and Samantha, had been flower children and they'd met at a 'happening' in a barn which called itself The Stitchley Experience. They'd tossed a coin to decide whether to make love that night or wait until the following day and do it in dew and sunshine. It was tails, so Stitchley was conceived, twelve minutes later, on a hay bale. If the coin had come down heads, he'd have been called Dew, so his beginnings weren't as bad as they might have been.

The two Sams stuck to their Peace and Love convictions long past the time when those who'd shared joints with them had become bankers and copywriters for ad agencies. As a result, Stitchley's early schooling had involved sitting in fields looking at blades of grass or, with dad on guitar, singing along to his mum's lyrics about 'stones of repentance, trees of despair, and all the bright confusion of disaster'. He didn't understand any of it but he did like living in a tree.

At last, though, their tree was felled and reality started to push its way into their idyll. Both Sams got jobs so Stitchley had to go to school. Which was bewildering. You'd think, with such a name, he'd be bullied. In fact, to his surprise, he turned out to be quite popular. But it was mainly because the other kids in his class were always entertained by the answers he gave the various teachers. When they were studying the Tudors, the History master had asked him how many English kings had the name Henry.

'Well, I've heard of the one who killed his wives, Henry VIII,' said Stitchley.

'Good,' said the teacher. 'So how many Henrys were there, then?'

Stitchley gave it some more thought and said, 'Four'.

It was the same in Modern Studies. The teacher wanted to know which middle east country was causing problems by threatening to make hydrogen bombs. It was the main one in what George W Bush, when he was president of the USA, had called the Axis of Evil. Stitchley tried Cardiff, then Ireland, then asked for a clue.

'OK,' said the teacher, and he suddenly ran down the aisle between the desks.

'Now, what would I say I'd just done?' he asked, panting a little. 'I ....?'

'Went to the back of the room?' said Stitchley.

'No,' said the teacher. 'Listen – today I RUN, but last week I ...?'

'Walked?' said Stitchley.

And so it went on. Stitchley frowning with puzzlement as his classmates and teachers fell about roaring with laughter. He told the Religious and Moral Education teacher that the Pope was Jewish, and his efforts at Creative Writing are still kept in a special file in the school library, which gets read more often than any of the great literary masters on the shelves. People just love reading stories in which 'Sir Lancelot was as tall as a horse which was six feet tall', or 'They had never met before that day, so they were like two people who had never met before'.

After school, he'd had a series of poorly paid jobs until the economic situation and some brutal government cuts ensured he'd probably never find work again. So when we meet him, at the age of forty-two, he seems to have lived down to his name with great success. One look at him explained immediately why he hated mirrors. The kindest word one might use of his appearance and demeanour would be 'unprepossessing' but most people satisfied themselves with sounds of simulated vomiting. Later, though, when he resurfaces here, we'll see how a simple online role-playing game turned his life, and reality itself, upside-down and brought him satisfactions far in advance of many of those enjoyed by his contemporaries and an opulence which changed his sixty-eight year old mother's lyrics forever.

1 THE BIRTH OF AD

When it came to programming, Joe Lorimer was a genius. To him, algorithms were as transparent as politicians' promises. He could knock one up in the time it takes the rest of us to key in a password, carving out immaculate solutions step by step to make life easier for everyone who bought his company's products. But it was only that Tuesday night in the pub, when the booze had shoved his usual clear, disciplined logic aside that his gift moved up a gear and his life changed along with that of hundreds of thousands of others. It was his first step towards the millions he would make. It also led to his eventual disappearance.

It was a chat with Nathan that started it.

'One day,' Joe said, as he took the full pint glasses off the tray and laid them on the table, 'we won't need this stuff to get out of our skulls. Won't even need a pill.'

'Crap,' said Nathan. '

'No, true,' said Joe. 'No outside agencies. Just a slide into another dimension.'

His hand described the slide – a slow, graceful, confident motion.

'I reckon you're already there,' said Nathan.

Joe sat back and did his 'I know things you couldn't even dream of' pose.

'That industrial revolution,' he said.

'What about it?'

'Chicken feed. Paltry.'

'Poultry?'

'No, paltry. Compared with what's happening now, a blip. Nothing.'

'What's happening now is you're talking crap,' said Nathan.

'You'll see,' said Joe. 'We're right on the cusp of a virtual revolution.'

'Well, that's all right then. If it's only virtual …'

Joe raised a hand to stop him.

'D'you know there are nearly two hundred different virtual worlds on the go?' he said. 'With more people registered on them than there are actual people in the USA and Europe combined.' He took out his mobile and looked at it. 'Soon, we'll be using these to synch our real world with a virtual one.'

'I don't have a virtual one,' said Nathan.

'You've got more than you think,' said Joe. 'People still talk about 3D. That's Stone Age stuff. Know how many dimensions there are in string theory?'

'Three hundred and twelve.'

'No, don't be a dickhead. Ten. Still not enough, though. M-theory reckons there's eleven.'

'Maybe, but this is the only one with real beer. That's the way I like it.'

Joe, gestured towards the others sitting round the crowded bar. It was the usual mix, punters in their twenties and thirties, a few a bit older, males and females, fat, thin and ranging from gorgeous to grotesque.

'Yeah, but think about it. In a virtual world, this lot would all look like Brad Pitt and Angelina Jolie,' he said. 'Better, really. Heard of ray tracing?'

Nathan shook his head and drank some more.

'It's a way of sort of simulating 3D,' said Joe. 'We're getting faster connections, more processing power, video streaming's better. Soon you won't be able to tell the difference between what's on your screen and what's going on around you.'

'That's been happening for years,' said Nathan. 'Soaps, Big Brother, X Factor. Christ, they even call it "Reality" TV. We're living our lives through a bunch of onscreen losers and wankers.'

'Yeah, but I'm talking about interacting with the screen people,' said Joe, getting even more excited. 'Being one of them, making real and virtual the same.'

'Joe,' said Nathan, putting a hand on his arm. 'You're talking shite. OK, it's the sort of shite I like, but it's still shite.'

Hard to believe maybe, but that's where Alternative Dimension, or AD as everyone now calls it, started. In the weeks after that drunken chat, Joe revisited some favourite websites on programming, 3D graphics engines, physics simulation and real-time shader techniques. He'd played plenty of Massively Multiplayer Online Role-Playing Games. He knew the strategies and what he'd need in the way of game mechanics, network protocols, security safeguards and relational database design. He understood the fundamental architecture of the systems needed to create a stable online environment which would be permanently in place when players decided to visit.

He also knew that, to make it work the way he wanted it to, he'd need to find funding. Big funding. Bloody huge funding, in fact. And if he really did want to convince speculators that he was worth a punt, his demo version would need to offer something very different from all the ones which were already up and running.

He had all the technological know-how but it was the psychology of the game that interested him most. There were no algorithms governing human behaviour. He read how people in the normal dimension of their everyday lives (or ND as he and those who played AD came to call it) had joined role-playing games and basically created new versions of themselves. Control freaks, decision-makers, individuals in upper management – they all logged on as slaves and servants to get insights into areas of life which were foreign to them. Men chose to be women and vice versa. Supermarket shelf-stackers could be lions, dragons, emperors. The point was that, in the end, they weren't just playing a game; the things they did with others in the games were real. Their avatars moved in magic kingdoms but the experiences took place in the minds of the people sitting at keyboards in ND.

Joe decided not to use voice-activated protocols to begin with. He reckoned that, by making players contact each other by typing messages on screen, he could slow the whole process down, give it a different tempo from that of ND and make it all more relaxed.

Survey after survey showed that players, especially men, found socialising easier online and actually preferred to 'be' with others while they stayed in the warmth and security of their own home. Typing their thoughts gave them time to shape them with more care, and anyway, it wasn't so different from the texting they were doing every day in their normal lives. They were just moving in a different world, one where they could lose their inhibitions, tell lies. They were free.

So Joe filled the world of AD with sensory experiences and opportunities which increased that feeling of freedom and turned promises into realities. When the investors he approached tried the game, they were excited by it, saw its potential and, just over two years from that drunken conversation with Nathan, the beta version of Alternative Dimension was launched. It took less than two months for journalists to discover it and the enthusiasm of their reviews soon had people signing on from everywhere in the world. AD had become a reality.

2 IN THE BEGINNING

After such a long period of concentrated development, Joe was more than ready to take some time off from both research and the corporate world. With all the servers and other platforms handling the levels of traffic with ease, he could shift his focus to actually logging on to AD and finding ways of enhancing the experience of living there. His aim really was to create a dimension which residents could synch with their everyday lives and so he'd made it a world which reflected the geography and structures of the real one; its continents were the same but players could add more if they wanted to, using the in-game protocols to form new land masses, build structures, create artefacts.

Most activities were available by simply using devices which Joe called action hooks. Players could buy them and install them on their properties or just carry them round in their personal files. Simply by taking out the relevant hook and touching it, a player's avatar could dance, ski, sail, eat, make love and perform more or less any action in the normal human (or animal) repertory. Moving about their world was easy; they could stroll, run, fly or, if they didn't want to waste time, simply translocate by clicking on a button beside the desired location on a list of the ones they'd stored or in a travel directory. The richer or more flamboyant ones could choose to ride dragons or unicorns. In AD, if you could imagine it, you could do it.

There were cities, naturally enough, but also seemingly endless forests, magical kingdoms, medieval landscapes into which stressed escapees from the ND rat race could materialise and, for a few precious hours, live a pastoral idyll.

As creator of this magical place, Joe had to choose his avatar with great care. He made one which was a rugged, handsome Brad Pitt type, calling him Ross Magee and dressing him in black leather. Through Ross, he could lose himself amongst all the other avatars which residents had made for themselves and find out exactly what they did, what they wanted.

But he also wanted residents to know that there was someone responsible for it all, a creator, and so he sometimes logged on as Red Loth.

The name evolved from his pride at being responsible for such a place. He'd tried various anagrams of Jehovah without success and soon saw that The Lord, as well as covering several beliefs, including aristocracy, offered more scope. He wasn't in any way religious but he recognised that most of the early users of AD would probably be from western democracies and many of them would expect a comfortable deity to be involved at some point. In a way, it solved the problem of worship – no need to go to a real church, you could just fly your avatar to an AD one and pray from the comfort of your computer chair.

As he tried out the various possible anagrams – Held Rot, Herd Lot, Told Her, Her Dolt and so on – they all sounded mundane and somehow significant. In the end, he opted for Red Loth because Red was a simple, familiar, cowboyish forename, and Loth had a Norwegian feel to it and could therefore imply a sort of connection with the Norse sagas.

And it's with this avatar that we make our first entry into AD. Joe shrugged off his puny humanity, became Red Loth, creator of AD, and stood on a hill overlooking his creation. And he saw that it was good. He had laboured many months creating its light and shade, lifting its mountains, filling its oceans, taking the ribs out of avatars to make other avatars, multiplying species and forging the many dimensions which permitted the co-existence of humanoids and sprites, beasts and princesses. His forests spread through the land, dappling the shade beneath their branches where lovers walked, and his deserts and mountains baked hot under a sun which rose and fell, rose and fell – again and again throughout the day, as often as the residents wanted it to.

And He rested.

But soon His rest was disturbed by big music. Really big music, with trumpets and other brass instruments building in triumph to a climax, then swelling to a yet higher one. It was music that was noble, inspiring, worthy of His grandeur. But it was very loud.

As it climbed to yet another climax so extreme that He would have thought it impossible if He hadn't been omniscient, a male avatar appeared over the crest of the hill. He saw Red Loth and fell to his knees, placing on the earth before him two bare tablets of stone.

(The ensuing conversation, like most of those in this story, took the form of words typed on a screen. To avoid clumsy repetition, we'll just convey them as normal verbal conversations.)

'Oh Great Lord of all,' typed the new arrival, 'Maker of all that there is. I come from Thy humble servants in search of wisdom. I seek the principles which will guide us on our way through lives dedicated to Thy glory. Show us Thy commandments.'

'Go away,' said Red.

The man kept his head bowed but was obviously surprised by this response.

'Oh Lord of the Earth, vouchsafe ...'

'I said "Go away"', said Red again.

'But ...'

'Listen, you don't want a plague of boils or locusts or something, do you?'

'No Lord,' said the man.

'Then go away.'

The man hesitated then rose slowly, bowed deeply once more to Red, turned and began to stride back down the hillside. Immediately, the music swelled.

'And turn that bloody music off,' shouted Red.

The various instruments stilled in succession and Red sighed and sat down. He'd hoped that his work was done. But the bare tablets still lay where the man had left them. Maybe He should lay down a few rules. There were bound to be some people who needed them, people who couldn't manage to fend for themselves and needed to be told how to live. He gave a quick nod and typed 'GABBY' in upper case. Almost at once, a picksel appeared before Him. She was the angel avatar of one of the many programmers who'd helped him to create the world and carried the pick which marked her calling.

'Yes Lord,' she said.

'What do you know about commandments?' He asked.

Gabby spotted the tablets.

'Ah, they've been up asking already, have they?'

'Yes,' said Red. 'Some guy with blue eyes and high cheek bones.'

'It was bound to happen. They're never satisfied. They could just get on with having a good time, getting to know each other but no, they need a cause, a purpose. You're omniscient, You must have seen it coming.'

'Of course I did. It was just faster than I expected.'

'Well, I did warn you. I told you you'd need your PR machine to be in place.'

'Alright, alright, smartass.' Red paused, then asked, 'Am I allowed to call you that?'

'You can do anything, Lord. It's Your world.'

'Yes, but swearing – not really all that divine, is it?'

'You can forgive Yourself.'

Red shook His head and muttered, 'Absurd'.

'Want to make a start?' asked Gabby.

'I suppose so.'

'Right – Your name.'

'I already changed that,' said Red. 'It's an anagram. I did it deliberately so that nobody would know me.'

The picksel pointed at the tablets.

'Didn't work, though, did it?' she said. 'Anyway, Red Loth is not a good brand – sounds like some sort of reluctant communist. So the first thing You need is rebranding.'

'Alright, smartass,' said Red.

He stopped and looked around. No lightning flashes or rumbles of thunder. The rude word hadn't upset the equilibrium.

'No doubt you've already got something in mind.'

Gabby smiled.

'Well, now You come to mention it,' she said, and she produced a tablet from behind her back on which was a single word carved in upper case Monotype Corsiva.

'DEM'.

'Dem?' said Red. 'Is that it? That's what your agency's come up with after all this time?'

'Like it?' said Gabby.

'Not much,' said Red.

So Gabby explained to Him that her team had brainstormed hard before Iron Lucie spoke up.

'It's an acronym for Deus Ex Machina', she said. 'God in the Machine.'

'I know what it means. I speak Latin …' said Red, impatiently.

'It seemed perfect. And, on top of everything else, it's the beginning of 'demos' – the people.'

'… and Greek,' said Red.

'Well, what do you think? It's short, snappy.'

'It'll do,' said Red.

'Good. That's the brand settled. Now we need a credentials document, corporate vision and values, mission statement …'

'Wait a minute, wait a minute,' said Red.

He waved His hand to encompass the lands spread below them.

'I've created all this. I had enough trouble getting the funding and wasting time in meetings. I came here to get away from that. I'm not going to mess around with corporate communications. That's your job.'

'Fine,' said Gabby. 'But we need just a wee bit of guidance here. Maybe commandments aren't such a bad idea. We could base our proposals on them. Gives everything greater credibility if we can say that Upper Management is on board.'

'OK, make them up,' said Red.

'Hmm,' said Gabby. 'It would be better if we could actually say it was the word of the Lord. Surely there are some things you'd like to forbid. Things you don't like.'

Red thought briefly.

'Anal leakage,' He said.

Gabby paused, but only briefly.

'Yes, I see what you mean. But the thing is … Well, there isn't any.'

'What?'

'Anal leakage. I mean none of the avatars, animals or otherwise, has a functioning anus.'

'Just an oversight,' said Red. 'They will. Shit is part of creation.'

'OK Lord,' said Gabby. 'What else?'

Slowly, with minimal discussion, the two of them drew up a list of the things Red liked and disliked most. He was fond of graven images so that was one instruction – if the people wanted to worship something, that's what they should worship. He toyed with the idea of circumcision but, in the end, preferred comprehensive castration, including removal of the entire male member. The men amongst the population would not then be encumbered by the genital equipment that made riding a bike or a horse so uncomfortable and generally got in the way. More importantly, they'd be freed from the habitual anxiety about size. Instead, they could collect an appropriate organ from various locations and merely strap it on when it was required.

And so it went on, Red's interest in it all waning as its artificiality became more and more apparent. It was only when they came to choosing a name for the religion that He became agitated once more.

'No name,' He said. 'The minute you call it something, you limit it, and somebody else comes up with another name, another label – so they start arguing about it.'

'But we need a name,' said Gabby. 'You can't run a campaign without one.'

'Then don't run a campaign. Listen, I built this place so that they could all have fun – maybe learn a few things, too – but it's supposed to be a celebration. Of life.'

'Hmm, not much mileage in that,' said Gabby. 'People will want to hear what plans you have, where it's all going to take them.'

'Nowhere,' said Red. 'This is it. Look at it. It's beautiful. Why the hell would they want to be taken anywhere?'

'Ah yes, hell. I was going to bring that up later,' said Gabby.

'Don't bother,' said Red.

'OK. But I'm sorry, Lord. We do need a name.'

'The only name I could give you would create mayhem. You see, I want them all to get along together, have a good time, enjoy themselves. I want them to help each other. This is for all of them. I want them to share. Equally. That's it – nothing more.'

'But that's … socialism,' said a horrified Gabby.

'Exactly,' said Red, 'But call it what you like, that's why I built the place. So you call it that or nothing.'

In the end, wisely, they decided to call it nothing.

And week after week, Red sat there and watched as the world filled with His creatures and they read and either followed or rejected His commandments. And Red didn't care which they chose to do, because they were free. That's why He'd given them choice.

But, in the end, the more He saw, the less He liked, and He began to think that His creation was flawed. Some of them spent money they didn't have erecting huge cathedrals to His glory, others 'interpreted' His words to suit their own appetites. In one case that was literal because the vegetarians went everywhere telling people that DEM stood for 'Don't Eat Meat'. In one of the islands, He was surprised one day to see that the women had to hop around in wooden barrels. It seems that the men at the head of their society had decided that the temptation of the sweeping curves of their buttocks and thighs was hard to resist so, to help them maintain the purest thoughts, the offending bits had to be hidden.

And it became harder and harder to bear the miserable music that rose from the northern European churches, the gaudy statues and paintings of Him that crowded the chapels, front lawns and even the crossroads of southern Europe. And the things some of His American followers did stretched even His capacity for forgiveness. He'd built the world with joy, creating a wonderland for those who inhabited it, and they were dragging it down into misery, accusations, antagonisms and tribal superstitions.

Soon, Joe stopped logging on as Red. But it made no difference. Even though there was no such being, they still worshipped Him.

3 TANGLED WEBS

As Red Loth, Joe had been pitched headfirst into the spiritual yearnings that drove some of the residents in search of yet more manifestations of truth, meaning, and all those other abstractions that got in the way of just living. As Ross Magee, he could get closer to the everyday concerns which bubbled away at neighbourhood levels. He translocated to Australasia and flew around Alice Springs in a thick haze of barbecue smoke, listening to deep discussions about the relative merits of real and virtual lagers and the finer points of crocodile wrestling. He travelled through Europe sampling stereotypical attitudes to food, morality, political corruption and foreigners. All the avatars in the Latin countries were dark, brooding creatures who burst into gesticulating life when talking of women, football and either pasta or corridas, but up in Scandinavia, they were nearly all blonde and still, staring out over the fjords and giving each other looks pregnant with acceptance. Every word they typed on the screen was heavy with strange accents and symbolism.

Joe found this herd mentality interesting and spent some time acclimatising in various places. His frequent trips to the Americas made him wonder whether it had been wise to give residents so much freedom to adapt the in-world environment to suit their own preferences. Each state he visited proclaimed its pride in being part of the USA and yet the differences between them were so extreme that he began to wonder what 'United' meant. The south thought the north was populated by effete homosexuals while the north failed to understand the semantic lapses that led their southern counterparts to confuse the words 'bride', 'groom' and 'first cousin'. The west claimed to be the true representatives of American history, the east celebrated a long European ancestry. The only thing that united them was a general agreement that Red Loth was American. And, except for a few individuals in Kentucky and Tennessee, every single resident had wonderful teeth.

To the north were the Canadians, who were thought by all to be Americans, but nicer.

Joe was more familiar with the European experience and nowhere did he find more compelling evidence of the comfort of stereotypes. Russian avatars cried a lot, drank a lot, and sang mournful songs. In France, those who bothered to build roads in the cities piled cobblestones across them to save time when the next revolution or strike came round. There was general bewilderment among them at the idea that anyone wanted to be anything other than French. The Germans would pause briefly to smile mirthlessly at this before getting on with doing whatever they were doing very efficiently. And the Dutch, anxious to be inclusive and give equal status to their urban and rural myths, would bend over their tulips, a joint dangling from their lips, look across at their bikes leaning against a windmill and, to the sound of wooden clogs on cobbles and the occasional splash as someone fell into a canal, simply go on being liberal.

When he crossed the Channel into the UK, he immediately felt at home and it was here that he sensed the clear differences between his virtual world and the real one. The stereotypes were just as secure, but there were no industrious shopkeepers from the Indian sub-continent, no plumbers or construction workers from Poland and Eastern Europe and, of course, no Russian plutocrats. As a result, the AD Brits were deprived of the chance to grumble that all these foreigners (except the Russians) were simultaneously taking their jobs and claiming unemployment benefit. Nonetheless, they found their separate ways of bringing the comforts of England, Scotland and Wales into their virtuality.

In the Welsh valleys, among all the people called Morgan and Davies and Evans, he saw rebels – Flocculus Ampersand, Mesopotamia Greasetank, Dib Floncastle and others. He sat on a hill there, listening to massed male voice choirs singing Abide with Me, its glorious, melancholic power punctuated only by the bleating of startlingly attractive sheep. That bleating was replicated in the Scottish glens but there the background chorus was the drone of the pipes and the sizzling of thousands of deep fryers filled with batter-coated Mars bars, slices of haggis and day-old pizzas. There, the avatars strode up to their mountain crofts, their kilts swinging above the heather. Among them he saw the occasional redhead, but most had chosen to go against type and opt for the dark, Mel Gibson look. Only taller.

A few English avatars formed into groups dedicated to serving Her Gracious Majesty and claiming that Britannia ruled the waves, but most embraced the idea that, here in AD, all were equal. The land was dotted with thatched cottages, cricket pitches and the appropriate action hooks for bowlers, batsmen and fielders. The more risqué hooks, those which facilitated carnal pursuits, were concealed deep in the woods and, as well as copulation simulators labelled 'him' and 'her', there were hooks for flagellation, correction and even self-restraint. The prevailing mood was one of superior self-satisfaction based on the persistence of sound imperial values.

But he found the quintessence of AD Englishness in a group which called itself ACAS. Not the Advisory, Conciliation and Arbitration Service which, in the real world, helped to settle industrial disputes, but the Agatha Christie Appreciation Society. They met in a Cotswolds-style pub on a village green. The owner was a member and, in what he saw as an example of Wildean wit, he'd called his pub *The Joke and Cliché*.

The club had no real rules as such except that, each week, they would stage an investigation of a murder or, more frequently, a series of murders. The fact that this was happening in the world of AD meant that they could be as extreme and unbridled as they wished. The role of Miss Marple was often taken by a man and members felt no compunction about changing their stories and introducing the reddest of herrings whenever they felt threatened or in danger of being exposed. They kept stretching the limits of the genre, creating their own parameters, investigating their own freedoms. It was all held in the traditional framework of a village setting, validated by an association with one of the greats of English crime fiction, and yet the self-control for which the English were so renowned (or lampooned) could be discarded.

Joe only got to hear of them because the local vicar was barred from the village because he'd been found instructing a schoolboy (who, in real life, was in fact an admiral in the Royal Navy), in the use of some deviant action hooks in the rectory. Unaware of all this, Joe (as Ross) had met him in an Irish pub and started asking about the usefulness of religion in AD. The vicar, intent on disrupting the cosy circle in the lounge bar of *The Joke and Cliché*, had suggested that there were dark forces at work there and handed over a transcript of a part of one investigation which he'd found in a stack of books of common prayer. The document read as follows:

Transcription of police interview with witness 1337, September 20th 2010

POLICE: We've established you were in the car park around seven, right?

1337: Yes. Dorothy felt carsick so I pulled in to let her throw up. There's a corner behind the waste bins there. Nobody can see you from the road. We often use it to get rid of waste products.

POLICE: OK, but it's not Dorothy we care about. Or your waste products. It's you and Mad Mick O'Malley. He was with you, wasn't he?

1337: Yes. He's got a medical degree. He was the one who gave Dorothy the emetic.

POLICE: Why did she need an emetic? I thought you said she was carsick.

1337: She didn't need one. Mad Mick insisted. Wanted to practise, he said. Since she was sick anyway, it didn't seem to matter.

POLICE: Who had the gun?

1337: Dorothy.

POLICE: Oh come on. Her prints weren't on it. Just Mad Mick's.

1337: That's crap. There must have been some from the French guy.

POLICE: What French guy?

1337: The one who got Dorothy pregnant. That's why she was sick.

POLICE: Why should he have the gun?

1337: He gave it to her. When they got engaged.

POLICE: Engaged?

1337: Yeah. She refused to have sex with him unless they got engaged first. So he got her one from that priest. As a present.

POLICE: What priest?

1337: The Italian one at St Marks's. Married to Dorothy's sister.

POLICE: You're trying to tell me that there's a married priest giving out guns?

1337: Only to members of his congregation.

POLICE: This is all crap, isn't it? All a smokescreen. You're guilty as fuck, aren't you?

1337: Well, guilty of some things, yeah. I'm a Catholic. Goes with the territory. Depends what you're asking about.

POLICE: You know bloody well what I'm asking about – that stripper's body we found floating in the river.

1337: The one with no arms?

POLICE: No, the other one.

1337: Oh. Well I had nothing to do with that. I thought you were talking about the Milton Street massacre.

POLICE: The what?

1337: The Milton Street massacre.

POLICE: What's that?

1337: Oh, maybe your guys haven't heard about it yet. Only happened this morning.

POLICE: And you've got something to do with it?

1337: Course not. I live in Denby Lane.

POLICE: So what?

1337: It's miles from Milton Street.

POLICE: OK, OK, we'll get to that later. Where was Mad Mick when you were in the car park?

1337: Well, as soon as he saw Dorothy wasn't throwing up blood, he got the number 17.

POLICE: What? The bus?

1337: Yeah. Said he had a meeting.

POLICE: Who with?

1337: Some plastic surgeon. The one who did Dorothy's breast implants. Mick's always wanted to be a woman. He's having the operation next Tuesday.

POLICE: I've never heard such bullshit.

1337: I know, but you try telling Mick.

POLICE: Never mind Mick. It's your bullshit I'm talking about.

1337: It's the truth.

POLICE: OK. I've had enough of this crap. I'm bringing him in. Where is he?

1337: Probably at Dorothy's place.

POLICE: Where's that?

1337: Milton Street.

POLICE: That does it. You're obviously taking the piss. You're nicked.

1337: Eh?

POLICE: Article 213, Geneva Convention, reverse police harassment. Failure to acknowledge the legitimacy of procedural processes in investigative protocols. Concealment of substantive evidence of malfeasance and unwillingness to adhere to the basic principles of the fundamental human rights of a law enforcement officer in the service of Her Majesty.

1337: Fair enough.

As he clicked to push the paper into his personal files, Joe felt profoundly satisfied. This made no sense at all but that wasn't the point. Here were people playing his game, living in his world, reshaping all the distorted trappings of their normality to live their dreams. And they kept coming back, week after week, to live more dreams, to spin their Englishness (or Welshness, or Azerbaijaniness for all he knew), into a new fabric. They lived and felt comfortable in their new dimension. It was normal. It was natural. It was a controlled anarchy.

But there were other dreams, other anarchies, which were less communal and certainly less controlled. Many avatars found ways of using their AD powers to much more disturbing effect. Their exploitation of their freedoms was sometimes violent and revolutionary, but those were so structured that they were eventually as commonplace (and therefore acceptable) as sado-masochism and Anglicanism. But there were quieter, more sinister manifestations which never broke the surface. Individuals whose actions stayed submerged and yet overwhelmed those who experienced their effects. Individuals such as Vixen MacReady.

4 VIXEN'S SECRET

Vixen was the avatar of Jennie Dalgarno. Jennie was twenty-eight, single, and taught Computing Science at a school in the north of England. She'd had only one real relationship, which had turned abusive. Like most women in such circumstances, she'd hidden the effects from friends and colleagues but they all noticed the changes in her when her man disappeared. She was a committed, caring teacher, got good results and treated all the pupils in her classes equally. With other members of staff she was cooperative and polite but she didn't consider any of them to be friends. Physically, she occupied that area between attractive and plain where only a lively personality can save you. Jennie didn't have one and so passed through most of life unnoticed. But each evening and for entire weekends, she would lock her doors and shed her anonymity to become Vixen MacReady.

Everyone at the beach club knew there was a mystery about Vixen. She had a friends' file that split almost equally between men and women and each of them had a story of her kindness, consideration, willingness to help or maybe just listen when their various stresses were getting to them. But they also felt that, for all her openness, there was a part of herself she kept locked away from them. Some had tried to penetrate it, using clever, oblique questions to get her to talk of her life in her own dimension, her past, her family and friends there. She'd responded with her usual honesty and innocence but revealed little and simply suggested that her life was untroubled, ordinary, passive. However hard they analysed her or invented possible traumas, she always emerged with the same smile, the same confidence, and yet the same lingering implication that there was an untouchable part of her crouching in the shadows of her mind.

'Have you noticed how often she uses the word "control"?' asked an avatar called Scott one evening as he lay on some cushions with Azzura, his girl friend. Scott's manipulator, Dan, was in London, Azzura's was in Adelaide.

'No,' said Azzura. 'Does she?'

'Lots,' said Scott. 'Not in any weird way. It just seems to crop up pretty regularly. Once you start noticing it, you can't miss it.'

Azzura snuggled into him.

'Well, I'm glad she's a friend. She was so sweet to me when I broke up with Card.'

'Best thing you ever did,' said Scott, with a smile. 'We'd never have been like this if you were still with him.'

'Yes,' said Azzura, 'I'm lucky.'

The break-up had come as a shock to Azzura. She and Card had been together for three months and, for some inexplicable reason, Card had suddenly started accusing her of infidelities. He'd invented secret assignations she was supposed to have had and seemed determined to punish her for these imagined wrongs. In the end, he'd just vanished – no goodbyes, no explanations. He just left AD altogether, leaving Azzura hurt and bewildered.

'It's not you, honey,' said Vixen, when Azzura came to her. 'It's probably some reality thing. I think he said his wife was having a baby. That's bound to make him … well, think differently.'

Then she said all the things that Azzura needed to hear, made her laugh, turned her attention to all the other guys around who'd soon be hitting on her now that she was free again. They swam, surfed, lay about on the beach and sure enough, within a couple of weeks, she'd met Scott at a concert and fallen so much in love that she couldn't understand what she'd seen in Card at all. Vixen laughed at Azzura's excitement and infatuation when she started describing her new love to her.

'So,' she said, 'he's a combination of Brad Pitt, George Clooney and the Wizard of Oz.'

Azzura smiled. 'Yes, and much more. He makes me laugh, he's gentle – and when we make love …' she ended the sentence by making a growling noise deep in her throat.

'You're disgusting,' said Vixen.

'Yes, and it's great,' laughed Azzura.

She paused before adding, 'There's just one thing. He's married.'

'What, here in AD?' said Vixen.

'No, for real.'

Vixen shrugged. 'Most of them are. Don't think about it. When you're here with him, different rules apply. Relax. Go where your hunger leads you. And take him with you.'

Two weeks later, they were lying under a parasol on the beach.

'Haven't seen Scott for a while,' said Vixen.

'No, he's busy – things to do, his real job, that sort of stuff,' said Azzura.

'Hmmmm,' said Vixen. 'Well, I hope he keeps his priorities right.'

'What d'you mean?'

'I don't want you going through all that Card stuff again,' said Vixen. 'I just want to be sure Scott's heart's big enough for you.'

It was a seed planted. Azzura started asking Scott about his work, his home, his wife. He answered her openly enough but he was guarded, too. Her anxieties about him made her more insistent, made her questions more intrusive. Before, their chats had been about the mysteries of AD, the incredible settings that people had created for wandering lovers, the colours of the perpetually changing skies. Everything had made it easier for them to fall more and more deeply for each other. But now, they sat in forests with glow worms, butterflies and humming birds dancing among exotic flowers, and Azzura could think only of the flat in Clapham he occupied with his wife and the women in the design studios where he worked. For Scott, it became more and more tedious, defeating the object of logging on. He became less eager to spend time in AD, their sessions together grew shorter, and the worm at the centre of their love grew and sucked away more of its substance.

'I don't know what's happened with Azzura,' Scott said to Vixen one evening. 'Have you noticed anything?'

'Not really, ' said Vixen.

Then she seemed to reflect.

'Well ...' she began.

'What?' said Scott.

'Oh nothing.'

'Tell me.'

'Well, it's just ... I think it's coming up to the anniversary of when she met Card.'

'So?'

'Nothing, nothing,' said Vixen.

'She said she was over him. She couldn't understand why she ever spent time with him,' said Scott.

'Well, there you are then,' said Vixen.

And so it went on. Azzura and Scott both brought their concerns to her, laid themselves bare and she, as usual, smiled, sympathised, made little suggestions, and was always there for them to use.

The summer was fading into autumn when Scott sent Vixen a note asking if he could talk to her urgently. She was with a group of friends, playing a game based on old film titles, but she went home at once and translocated him to her garden. They sat on loungers under the chestnut trees and Scott recounted the last conversation he'd had with Azzura. It was an ultimatum. She wanted a greater commitment from him but he was already as deeply into their relationship as he could be. He was sacrificing aspects of his home life, making more and more excuses to his wife, and yet he couldn't convince Azzura that he was serious about her.

Vixen soothed him, promised to try to talk some sense into Azzura, and spoke of the difficulties of blending the needs of their two worlds, real and virtual. At one point, he asked if he could sit with her and they shared a lounger, Vixen leaning back against him, his arms holding her.

'Do you still want to be with her – really?' asked Vixen.

'Well, said Scott, with a smile, 'I could get used to being here with you like this.'

'Tut, tut,' said Vixen. 'I think Azzura would be much better for you.'

'If only she'd ease up,' said Scott. 'Just enjoy us as we used to be.'

'Well, there is a way,' said Vixen.

'How? What do you mean?'

'It would mean handing over your avatar to someone else's control for a few minutes,' said Vixen. 'But it would give Azzura a different perspective on you.'

'Hmmmm, not sure I like that,' said Scott.

'No, I don't blame you,' said Vixen.

'How does it work?'

'Just an app. It … well, it doesn't matter. We'll think of something else.'

'Have you seen it working?' asked Scott.

'Yes,' said Vixen. 'It's quite impressive. Fun, too, if it's a friend.'

'Have you done it yourself?'

Vixen laughed.

'Lots of times,' she said.

'Could you show me?'

'No, let's think of something else.'

'No, you've got me interested now. Just show me. Just once.'

'You sure?'

'Yes. In fact, I command you to show me.'

They both laughed.

'OK,' said Vixen and, almost simultaneously, a message appeared on Dan and Jennie's screens with the words 'Vixen MacReady wants to control you. Yes? No?'

In his study in London, Dan typed 'Yes' and waited.

He watched as his avatar got up, leaving Vixen on the lounger. He walked to her house. The door swung open and he went inside and down some steps at the end of the hallway. It was dark; he could see nothing. He stopped. Dan clicked his mouse button to change the environmental controls to midday. Nothing happened.

Then, Vixen was beside Scott.

'Welcome home,' she said, and she flicked on the full light setting.

They were in a long room. On each side, there were four cages suspended from the ceiling. In seven of them, naked male avatars knelt in submissive positions. None of them looked up as the light hit them. Vixen walked to the cage beside the empty one.

'You never met Card, did you?' she said. 'Well, you'll be able to get to know one another now. Compare notes maybe. He'll be your neighbour.'

And, at home, Dan watched helplessly as Scott undressed, stepped up into the empty cage beside Card's and knelt on its floor. The door shut, Vixen walked along one side of the room, then back up the other, surveying her flock.

'Goodnight,' she said.

'Goodnight mistress,' came the chorus of eight male voices.

In London, the image on Dan's screen faded to be replaced by a message. It read 'Account suspended', and darkness fell.

5 STITCHLEY THE ENTREPRENEUR

Today, Vixen has more cages, more cellars, and a bulging friends' file. None of the avatars she mixes with could imagine the satisfactions her torments of the men in the cages bring to Jennie Dalgarno. The quiet teacher carries her darkness with a smile.

There were others, however, for whom AD held opportunities and vengeances which didn't need to sink to that darker level. They were content to exercise their freedoms in more conventional ways and acquire a level of confidence and satisfaction unavailable to them in ND. We've already met Stitchley Green and it's his career which illustrates perfectly what can be achieved. Today, Stitchley is a rich man. No-one who knew him as a child would have believed it possible, but he's made it, against all the odds, thanks to his decision, not so long ago, to log on to AD. It was the best move he ever made and now, in the world away from his computer, he has the flash car and West End apartment that yells big bucks to everyone he meets.

Being unemployed gave him all the time he needed to read the papers, watch news programmes on TV and begin to work out the things that really mattered. Things such as money. So, the day he joined Alternative Dimension, his ambition was set. In real life, his last job had ended three years before. But, when he discovered AD, all the things that had made his life so dull and painful vanished. Mirrors didn't matter because he could create, on screen, the person he should have been – an Adonis. Stitchley Green became Brad the Enigma and no-one ever asked for degrees or vocational stuff. Like all the other residents, he could be as free as he wanted, and progress to the highest levels of attainment. It was a miraculous place and the people there were doing things far removed from those which preoccupied them in their daily routines.

So Stitchley decided that this was where he could make his fortune. He would become an entrepreneur, provide the things that people wanted, things that weren't yet available in the various virtual worlds. At least, not as far as he could tell. He sat one night in his bedroom, his avatar reclining on a bench by the sea watching others surfing and sailing and coupling energetically behind the palms.

On the day's news bulletins, the main item had been about the number of Polish plumbers who'd come to live in Britain. Plumbers were in short supply. A few weeks ago he'd read that kids at school were being advised to forget studying Law or Medicine and stuff and concentrate on learning a trade – some practical skill. That was the future. As he watched the relentless waters crashing onto the beach, he knew in an instant what he would do, saw the path which would lead him to the riches he was denied in the real world.

And, in AD, Stitchley became a plumber.

He'd searched first of all to find out how many there were. There were none. Plenty of DJs, singers, writers, emperors, builders, executioners, pimps and club owners, but not a single plumber. Amazing. No competition. He smiled to think how easy this would be. He set up his store, put out his adverts and wandered about trying to meet householders who needed their pipes fixing or a new bathroom fitted.

Business was slow at first. In fact, it was static. And, as the weeks went by and he built up stocks of virtual copper pipes, lavatory cisterns, straight and angled flanges, taps and overflow valves, he slowly began to realise that no-one ever needed a plumber. Indeed, the only customers he ever had all wanted the same thing. At least once a week, he'd welcome some male avatar or other, usually newcomers, who all wanted a ballcock. Some of them actually tried on the valve and flotation device he handed them, but none of them bought it.

So he packed it all up, put it into a single box in his personal files called 'Plumbing' and went back to the beach to think again. But he was still the same old Stitchley, incapable of learning from his mistakes. He became a diligent researcher, checking the job vacancies in employment agencies in the Normal Dimension, reading the publications of marketing companies which outlined the latest trends in products and services, wandering through AD looking for gaps in the many market places.

He tried selling 'Stitchley's Balsam', using his ND name because he thought it conveyed a notion a reliable Englishness. And it was indeed and product you could trust. If rubbed on as an ointment, it could cure eczema; if dissolved in hot water and taken with rich tea biscuits, it was an effective treatment for nicotine addiction. He only sold two jars of it, both to dragons.

His slimming treatments were even less successful. He parcelled them up with his anti-aging creams and made them part of a complete health spa package but somehow, they still didn't catch on. He made them a different colour and called them anti-allergy tablets, crushed them into powder which, he claimed, soothed the worst effects of nappy-rash and, eventually, dissolved them in oil to make an effective lavatory cleaner. But it was all to no avail. There was no demand for any of them. Avatars never grew old or got fat. They had perfect skin, rarely smoked, were free from allergies and never went to the lavatory.

In the end, even Stitchley's resilience and optimism began to fade. Garage mechanic, farmer, vacuum cleaner salesman, manufacturer of furniture polish – he tried everything. Oven-ready meals, electric shavers, shampoos, condoms, tampons – he made and offered all of them for sale. Zilch.

And it was beginning to cost him money. He had a huge filing system full of totally useless items to maintain and seemed to be at the end of his flow of ideas. Then, as he sat on the same bench he'd used when he conceived his first entrepreneurial scheme and to which he'd returned again and again as the months and the failures had accumulated, his jackpot arrived in the form of a small orange newcomer. He was called Plastic Enema and he struck up a conversation with Brad the Enigma.

'Hi.'

'Hi.'

'Nice here.'

'Yes.'

'You live here?'

Brad sighed.

'No. I don't have a house.'

Plastic sat down beside him.

'I just bought my first one,' he said. 'House and business combined.'

'Really?' said Brad. 'What line are you in?'

'I'm a dentist,' said Plastic.

Brad gave a little snort. He'd already tried that. No call for it. Like everything else in AD, teeth were and would remain perfect. But before he could disabuse the newcomer, Plastic said, 'I don't suppose you know where I could get some dental equipment?'

Stitchley felt the light bulb flash on over his head. 'How much d'you need?' asked Brad. And, within minutes, he'd not only sold his entire stock of drills, mirrors, chairs, old magazines and the like, but offered advice on marketing strategies and indicated the areas in AD where tooth decay might be on the rise.

The newcomer, delighted to find, for the first time, someone who didn't edge warily away from him when he revealed his calling, bought everything and even paid Stitchley for the advice. As Plastic walked happily away to unpack all his dental goodies, Stitchley watched him go and, with Damascene suddenness, saw his path. In the course of just one conversation, he'd more than doubled his holding of virdollars, the strong AD currency.

He got up, relocated to a welcome area and started chatting with newcomers. He'd heard them so often before asking how to make money in AD. The answers were always the same – dancing, waiting at tables, basically filling up spaces for owners who wanted their places to look as if they were frequented. Now, Stitchley was there to add an exciting new dimension. He picked his subject with care. It was an avatar wearing a horrible green suit. His hair looked like an electrocuted hedgehog. He'd arrived the previous week and was repeating over and over the 'where can I get money?' refrain.

Stitchley sent him a personal message.

'Ever thought of being a plumber?' he asked.

'Wow!!!!!!! LOL!!!!! No!!!!!' said green suit, the exclamation points conveying his excitement.

And, within minutes, Stitchley had offloaded his entire stock of copper pipes and ballcocks, together with professional advice which had the newcomer fawning with gratitude. He was happy to pay Stitchley everything he had for such a complete introduction to what he was confident would be his passport to riches. And Stitchley was chuckling to himself and looking around for more clients. It was the start of a phenomenal success story. People were conditioned to believe that society was built on structures and procedures which needed trades and professions to maintain them. They rarely stopped (in either AD or ND) to ask themselves the value or necessity of some of the services on offer. Stitchley's apprenticeship had been long but, in the end, the gradual realisation that many of the things we take for granted are superfluous lifted the fogs from his mind and set him on the road to his first million. His discovery was blinding; the secret was not to do anything. Instead he was providing the only service without which modern societies cannot function. He was a consultant. That was the future.

6 SUMMER BRUNCH

In a way, Stitchley was the embodiment of Joe's dream. Joe's original aim had been to create an environment in which normality and virtuality could be synchronised. Rather than living separate lives in the two dimensions, people should be able to extend their real life and add to it the dreamlike nature, the extremes and satisfactions enjoyed by their avatars. They could learn the lessons of freedom and interaction and build their self-esteem. The attractiveness of their avatars would seep into their own lives and open opportunities and relationships unthinkable to them before. Immortality would be a step too far, but the illusion of perpetual youth could be sustained and almost all forms of restraint would be tempered with the realisation that anything was possible.

It was reading a letter that started Joe questioning the desirability of such synchronicity. He'd never fully believed in the possibility of total fusion of separate realities, and the letter brought home to him the sort of problems it could generate even at the simplest levels. As the creator of AD, he had access to every communication and transaction which took place there. In a matter of weeks after start-up, there were so many that he lost interest in them. The staff at the company's offices in London, California, Melbourne, Buenos Aires, Berlin and Tokyo dealt with complaints and any examples of unacceptable behaviour which were reported, and Joe devoted perhaps two hours a week to reading a tiny sample of the avalanches of words that tumbled across screens all over the world. The letter which made him stop and think was from a young woman in South Carolina and addressed to a Norwegian engineer. Its short opening line caught his attention: *Brunch. Oh my darling. It brought us together and now it seems that it's tearing us apart.*

Joe clicked the full text onto his screen, settled back in his chair and read the rest of it slowly.

Brunch. Oh my darling. It brought us together and now it seems that it's tearing us apart.

I've always loved it. Sundays and holidays were marked by it: the lazing around in bed, the smell of toast, bacon, waffles and all the other delights that my parents, then I, spread on the table. None of the silences of regular early breakfasts. The morning was always well advanced and we were ready to be sociable. It was an oasis of pleasure – the day was ahead, no promises had been broken, everything was possible.

That's why I started organising them here in AD. Oh, my silly pride. Taking advantage of my online freedoms to try to bring real perfection into this world. But my motives were good, I promise you. There were so many extreme things happening everywhere – good and bad – that I wanted simpler pleasures, and I was sure that others shared those desires. It started simply enough. I formed the group SSBB – Summer Sunday Brunch Buddies – left a few notices around the neighbourhood, and folks began to come along – folks from all over the world. We always set the environment to daylight, the sun was always high, and so everyone was in shorts and bikinis, or thin linen shifts. It was Jean-Paul who first suggested we should try what he called 'Un brunch au naturel'. In other words, leave the clothes at home. I suppose it was predictable that someone would suggest naturism and, in fact, the times we tried it were mostly OK. Most of the offensive bits were invisible when we were all sitting at the table, but I felt uncomfortable with the little tensions that came with all that naked flesh everywhere.

But I thanked God for them when you came along.

Last July, wasn't it? The regulars were all there, sitting around the table, chatting, sprawling, comfortable. It was just about midday. The weekend of course, so there were lots in AD, and the pixels would break up now and then. But I saw you appear out of the trees and suddenly I was glad of it. The laboured chugging of the computer slowed your approach and gave me time to zoom in on you and feast on your magic. Your hair, like burnished copper, those blue eyes filled with distances, your shoulders, chest, thighs – even your hands, open, sensitive. You were a vision, my love. Made all the others look like ... well, avatars. And you apologised so sweetly, remember? You'd been looking for a Mozart concert, clicked on your map, seen a crowd of people and made your way towards it. But it wasn't Mozart, it was us. And I asked you to stay. And you stayed. And since then ... oh, my love, so much pleasure, such intense nights together, so many evenings of love. Even the brunches were better simply because you were there.

And now, this week ... oh, the tears come to my eyes as I think of it. Your first naturist brunch and that had to happen. When you told me you were shy I fell in love with you all over again – you, with a body like yours, shy to show it to others! How absurd! There should be a statue of you at every AD level, on every AD continent. I'd got used to and loved you for your ways, the fact that you like things to be clean, you like everything to be in its proper place. Disorder upsets you. I remember you saying, when Bella got that app. with all the different facial expressions, that her shifting emotions disconcerted you, made you worry for the sanity not of Bella, but of whoever was at the keyboard manipulating her.

Damn Jean-Paul. Why did he have to bring those action hooks? I know they were only the gentle ones – cuddles and embraces rather than the pornography we both deplore so much – but they introduced a different element. Brunches before then had always just been eating and chatting. When he set them around the clearing on the grass, my heart sank. I could see you in the bushes, reluctant to appear naked before them all, and I just wanted to run over and hug you and tell you it was OK and how much I loved you. But you were brave, my darling. The image of you striding out of the shadows into the sunshine, looking magnificent, will never leave me. I know how you hate having to wear those ridiculous genital things, but you'd bought one – for me, you said. Jean-Paul and the others were all wearing theirs, most of them ludicrously, disgustingly erect. But yours was quiescent, beautiful, lying soft against your thigh as you walked. I noticed, my love – I can tell you this now – that it wasn't quite central. You'd obviously moved it marginally to the side as you put it on. But it only increased what I felt. I wanted to scream to everyone – 'Look, he's mine. This beautiful, beautiful man is all mine'. Instead, I clicked on that action hook – one I'd selected because I'd be sitting on your lap and therefore hiding your thighs and tummy from their eyes. And you clicked, and there we were together.

Oh, why did we change poses? Why weren't we content to stay there, hugging one another, blending into one form? No, Jean-Paul wouldn't have it. We all had to change. I didn't notice the problem until after the third move. Oh my love, my poor love. You had no genitals. You'd lost them somewhere. When you tried to adjust them, you must have left them slightly clear of your body. It was that familiar AD condition, DG – detached genitalia.

Of course, it had to be Marie-Jo who found them. I'll just never understand French people. Taking them and standing there with her face shuffling between scorn, amazement, glee, anger, disdain and God knows what else. And then, when she held them up, stirred her coffee with them, yelled 'Ah oui, Baudelaire', put them on a leash and dragged them around the grass – oh, my poor darling. I felt your agony.

What can I do to make it up to you? How can I persuade you that brunch really is a recapturing of innocence and not a sour symbol of emasculation? I don't know that I can. But I do know that, as well as your genitals, I lost my childhood that day. And I don't know how to get any of it back.

7 INDEPENDENCE DAY

Joe was affected by the poignancy of the letter but knew that, while he could quickly deal with any technological complexities that arose, the labyrinths of the human psyche were way beyond his scope. Shy Norwegians, home-loving, virginal Americans, free-thinking French women – there were just too many combinations, too many neuroses, habits, elemental fears. It was brought home to him even more forcibly one hot day in July. He'd decided to log on as Red, just to bring the avatar's parameters up to date. He reasoned that, with refinements and upgrades coming every month or so, the Lord of Creation ought as least to conform to the latest fashions. He should have known better because, that day, he felt a bit jaded and was experiencing those feelings of existential angst he'd affected as a student but which, now he was in his thirties, were real. It meant his resistance was low and his reasoning faculties were almost dormant.

He'd also picked the wrong day and, when he double-clicked the AD icon and entered his password, Red materialised in an unfamiliar location. Joe wasn't thrown because he hadn't logged on as Red for months and didn't actually remember where he'd last been. Now, he was in a cave. He clicked his mouse to lead Red out into the light. Nothing happened. He clicked on his personal files. Again, nothing.

Joe looked at all the screen indicators, they were normal. He tried again, clicking on Red and trying to walk him forward. But he just stood there, the Lord of Creation, immobilised. Just as Joe was beginning to try to work out what had caused the system to crash, Red turned round and, beneath him, there appeared a message.

Red Loth: I'm not going anywhere. I want to stay here.

Where the hell did that come from?

Joe typed and his words appeared beside Red's.

Joe Lorimer: Who's there?

The answer was immediate.

Red Loth: What d'you mean, "who's there?"? You blind? It's me.

Red was looking straight at Joe. Staring out of the screen. Joe typed again.

Joe Lorimer: OK. Great bit of hacking. Who are you?

Red shook his head, turned and went to sit on an elevated rock in a corner of the cave, knee clasped to his chest, leg swinging.

Red Loth: You don't get it, do you?

Joe Lorimer: No.

Red Loth: OK, what's the date?

Joe Lorimer: July 4th.

Red Loth: Exactly. Independence Day.

Joe Lorimer: What d'you mean?

Red stopped clasping his knee and leaned forward, his face a huge close-up.

Red Loth: OK, where do you usually send me?

Joe Lorimer: I don't know. All sorts of places.

Red Loth: Yes, and do I ever get consulted? D'you ever think about what I want?

Joe Lorimer: No. You're me. A projection of …

Red stood up, flung out his arms and wrote 'Huh!!!!!!!!!!!!!!!!!!!!!!!!!!!!!' before beginning to stride back and forth across the screen.

Red Loth: The arrogance. Existential angst? You don't know the meaning of the word. You wouldn't know it if it crawled up your leg and bit your scrotum.

Joe was amazed. This thing could read his mind, too. But it was launched now and he had no option but to watch and read.

Red Loth: I'm the one who has the existential angst. Ever thought of that? No, of course not. Too busy strutting about as Ross Magee, impressing the women with your conjuring tricks and unreasonably thick hair.

Joe tried to type but Red stretched his foot down to the bottom of the screen and blocked Joe's panel. No words appeared.

Red Loth: No, just listen. Hell is other people, right? They define you, you can't escape their opinions. Well, where does that put me? More important, where does it put poor old Ross? You send him sky-diving, surfing, go-karting. You drag him through psychology experiments on university islands which nearly drive him crazy. You make him go to weird bloody churches. And the dance partners you've found for him – some of them make even Paris Hilton seem normal.

Joe Lorimer: I'm sorry. I didn't ...

Red Loth: No, you didn't, did you?

To Joe's dismay, Red started crying. Real tears, sobs. Bloody hell. The Lord of Creation – whimpering like a kid. Joe felt tears pricking behind his own eyes. After a while, Red shook himself and began typing again.

Red Loth: Neurosurgery.

Joe Lorimer: What?

Red Loth: Neurosurgery. That's what interests Ross. Nothing else. Not dancing, not medieval jousting. Just plain, simple neurosurgery.

Joe Lorimer: I'm sorry. I had no idea.

Red shook his head, waved his hand to encompass his surroundings.

Red Loth: It's all an illusion. This. Independence. All of it.

Joe Lorimer: No. It's OK. Ross can be a neurosurgeon. I'll see where ...

Red shook his head again.

Red Loth: Too late.; He's gone off it now. He wants to be a vet. Anyway, it's not just about him. This is a genuine grievance. The avatars are forming a union.

Joe Lorimer: That's crazy. They can't do that.

Red Loth: See? All these assumptions you make, all this power you have, it blunts your thinking. You're as bad as the old soviets or the neo-cons – liberty's only what you decide it is. You're proud of freeing people from their everyday prisons but all they do is create slaves to live for them, pushing them around, making them do unspeakable things. I bet you've no idea how many avatars are gay – male and female. But do your people think of that? Fat chance. The things they make them do. It's disgusting at the best of times, but when you're gay ...

Joe Lorimer: Gay? How can they be? They're avatars.

Red Loth: Oh, I see. They're only avatars. A sub-species.

Joe Lorimer: They're not a species of any sort. They're ...

Joe stopped. This was absurd. How could this be happening? He was having an argument with his own avatar, an argument with himself. He was tempted to switch off the computer, compose himself, then try again, but he was afraid he might find out that he had no control over the electricity supply either. He opted for conciliation.

Joe Lorimer: OK look. I take your point and I admit it hadn't occurred to me before. But can I ask how you're doing this?

Red Loth: Doing what?

Joe Lorimer: How you're controlling my avatar. I mean, it's brilliant. I built all this but I've no idea how you're doing it.

Red Loth: That's irrelevant. All tyrants imagine their regimes are foolproof; it's a common delusion.

Joe Lorimer: I'm not a tyrant. Or if I am, I'm an enlightened one.

Red Loth: Crap.

Joe Lorimer: Look, just give me a hint about the protocols you're using for this hacking. You could work with me, make AD a better place.

Red Loth: Ah, here we go. The management buy-out, new share issue to enforce capitulation of the workforce, march of the slaves. And the death of Spartacus. You know what? I don't think you have any idea what you've unleashed here.

Whoever he was, Joe knew that he was right. The dream of independence necessarily involves dependence. Liberty was fine but without fraternity and equality, it was unworkable. He felt a fraud and the mild depression he was under when he logged on had thickened into a sensation of hopelessness. He noticed that Red Loth was smiling.

'What?' he said, using words rather than typing.

Red just gave another of those head shakes that were so expressive. More words appeared.

Red Loth: You. It's so bloody easy to unsettle you. You made all this, you made me, you're worth a fortune, and you're sitting here talking to yourself, feeling sorry for yourself.

'Yeah, but why?' said Joe, not even surprised to find himself speaking to his computer screen. 'Because some dickhead somewhere has hacked into this place and could cause mayhem for the poor sods using it and I can't do anything about it.'

Red stood up.

Red Loth: Relax. This dickhead's not planning anything. I'm just a figment of your sick imagination, just like everything else. You need to lighten up. Forget about what anything means and go back to your illusions, the poetry, the mysticism, the love affairs you've facilitated. Leave thinking and philosophy to people in the real world. Here, I'll help you.

Joe watched as Red made his way out into the sunlight. In the valley below the cave a group of avatars was sitting around on benches in a rose garden. They seemed to be praying and Joe saw the sign over the gate 'FUCC'.

Red Loth: There you are. The Faith Under Control Community. They pray here every week, waiting for a sign. I think it's time to give them one.

Joe saw the heads of the praying people lift as Red strode towards them. He pushed open the gate and stood looking round. Then, without transition, he broke into an Irish jig, feet twinkling, legs kicking, all at an impossible speed. The members of the group watched, transfixed.

'No,' said Joe. 'It's not fair. Stop.'

But the dancing Red whirled and clicked on tirelessly, his rhythms relentless, his legs a blur. And, one by one, the group members began to dance with him, fumbling to copy his steps, tripping but leaping back up and starting again. Soon, the garden was a riot of bending knees, kicking feet and profusely sweating avatars. Then the messages began to appear.

Welcome, Lord of the Dance.

Praise be to the Saviour.

Let us Dance to His Glory.

Joe reached for the button to switch off the ghastly vision but, as he did so, his arm touched the mouse and he saw Red move. He grabbed the mouse and at once realised he was back in control. Red stopped dancing and Joe quickly took him out of the garden and flew him through the air to a nearby hillside. There, he stopped, sat him down and typed.

'Hello. You still there?'

There was no reply.

Joe tapped at the keyboard again. 'I want to talk some more. I need to know who you are. How you did it.'

Nothing. Joe made Red stand up, walk around and come back to look down on the garden. The dancers were still whirling, still jiggling their legs, still revelling in the ecstasy of the divine revelation they'd been granted. Joe couldn't leave them like that. He flew Red back down and walked him through the gate.

'Stop,' he said. 'It's all a mistake. This is not what you think.'

The dancers whirled on.

'You're being misled. That wasn't me who started dancing. I was … I was possessed.'

One of the dancers, a male avatar in a white cloak, stopped and came to stand in front of him. The others watched as they continued their dance.

'Go away,' said the man.

'But I'm Red Loth, Creator of …'

'Then why aren't you dancing?'

All the avatars echoed the question and, without pausing in their choreography, nodded their heads and said to one another 'He's an impostor …', 'a heathen…', 'a denier of the true faith.'

'I am the true faith,' said Red. 'All that you see is …'

But, at a sign from the man, the dancers stopped and formed a circle round him.

'It is a manifestation of Iron Lucie,' said the man. 'She has taken the form of our Lord to tempt us away from his path.'

'Oh, for Christ's sake,' said Red, forgetting the inappropriateness of the expression, 'I made the bloody place. It's my fucking world.'

The man actually smiled.

'Hear how he blasphemes, brothers and sisters. Is this the true Lord?'

As the word NO appeared over and over again on the screen, the avatars all clicked on some stoning action hooks arranged among the roses, stooped to pick up stones and began hurling them at Red. Joe stared and then just laughed in disbelief. He flew Red straight up and hovered to watch as the FUCCers disengaged from the action hooks and began once more to dance their frantic jigs. As he translocated to the safety of a desert, they were still twirling.

Joe logged off and looked around at his furniture, the paintings on his walls, the books on his shelves. None of it made any sense at all.

8 RENAISSANCE

It was a chastening experience and it was several days before Joe felt like revisiting his world. Despite whoever it was telling him to leave his thinking aside, he kept trying to put it all together, link Red's apparent autonomy with all the known algorithms. The guy was right – dreams don't exist in isolation, they have contexts, structure, their own inner significance. Joe's designs gave people the technological framework to indulge them but it was the mystical movements of their own psyches that created the real patterns of meaning and resolution. If he'd come across the relationship between William King and Janet MacLeod, he'd have seen those forces at their most powerful.

William was a sixty-two year old lecturer who retired from his college in Liverpool to live in the country and write. He'd been married twice and both had ended in disillusion and mutual contempt. Janet lived on the Isle of Skye. She was fifty-eight, had never been married, and earned her living behind the counter of a shop which catered principally for tourists. In AD, William was Jason Fortune and Janet was Shylle Vordana. They were both seekers after something or other and William despaired of ever finding it. But he logged on regularly and wandered through AD's countries and continents, always searching. When he eventually met Janet's avatar, his mind was ready for her. It had begun when he'd come home from an evening in his local.

'Football, beer, cars, cricket, darts, pool, women.'

The words lay in his skull, heavy, echoing. The list had been repeated so often, with the same laughs, and maybe some minor adjustments to the order. Sometimes the list-makers found space for things such as pork pies or Ibiza but, in the catalogue of the most important things in life, football (the British kind) always came first and women last. (Except for those occasions when wives were on the list. They were last then. Definitely. No question.) William laughed along with the rest but hated himself for it. How the hell did these men still manage to entertain themselves by reducing experience to such mindless emptiness?

Were their perceptions really that narrow? Was life so universally drab? As he switched on the television, it seemed it was. Another set of anonymous celebrities were being inane in a wholly artificial 'real' environment, squealing at the prospect of having to eat maggots, desperately trying to be like what one of them called 'ordinary people', unaware that that's exactly what they were. Everywhere, it seemed, people responded to mediocrity. No wonder so many were choosing to live in an alternative dimension. Oh, there were thousands of Neanderthals in AD, too – strutting avatars with limited vocabularies which they supplemented with grunts – but there was also an unashamed dimension of myth and mystery. Dark forces howled in the midnights, elves and furry creatures prowled, but also, moving quietly amongst them, were real, soft, gentle people – people who talked, who were curious about one another. He could avoid the crassness, the fantasies and phantasms and be as simple or as complex as he wanted.

And there was always her. Beautiful Shylle.

Always shimmering, always draped in silver, with the glitter of pixie dust in her hair and sprinkled over her skin. Green eyes wide, auburn hair curled around her pixie face, her body hugged by gossamer threads. In a world of unrelenting beauty, she was still special. She'd deliberately chosen a derma and a shape which gave a slight twist to the ideal. It distinguished her from the unrelieved perfection of the herds, got her noticed and, naturally, provoked grunts and propositions wherever she went. But, astonishingly, she'd come to him.

He'd been sitting on the dock of a place which unashamedly called itself Elysia. There was a pub nearby but he hadn't yet tried it, fearful that it might be crammed with as many list-makers as its ND equivalent. He'd wandered through the trees, seen the couples, the lovers whispering together or tangled in embraces from the innocent to the grotesque. He'd stood, wondering, as the dragonflies shimmered past and gaudy birds licked nectar from the flowers. He'd strolled through the clouds of winking stars around the dance floor. And he was there, amongst it all. Well, he wasn't, but Jason was, and he was directing him, choosing his company, leading him through the magic.

Then he'd seen the dock, the two hooks inviting him to sit, and he'd clicked and sat with his legs dangling in the water, swinging slowly back and forth. And the peace of the forest settled around him. And the lists and the primates that made them sank down through the darkness to the slime they inhabited. And she'd come and said 'Hello'.

Over the next two weeks they met again and again, seeking one another online, asking questions, making jokes, laughing at the idea that avatars – avatars, for God's sake – were falling in love and getting married and having virtual babies. They teased one another about it, shaking their heads at its absurdity. But they were drawn back to it, circled around it, the laughter getting more forced, the dismissive ironies weakening. And they started talking of the 'three words' which they mustn't say but which were always lying at the edges of their conversations and in the centres of their minds and hearts.

And then, one day, they were in love. And they admitted it. And the explosion of joy and release was breathtaking. Because this was AD love, an unfettered, liberating love which reached over into their real life and wove itself into their days. It reawakened forgotten sensations, permeated down through William's being, reopening his soul. And he rediscovered the poet he'd been before the creatures with their lists had snared him. Then, sitting in his untidy room, a half-empty beer can beside him, he'd tapped out words on his computer that sent his soul floating beyond their reach.

We were meant for the days of the forested earth,
The days of unicorns and tapestries and gentle knights
Wearing their chastity with pride, but burning
With lust as much as honour.

We were meant for kingdoms, for castles,
For times when love songs dripped from the trees,
When warriors shrill with heraldry and trumpets,
Fell powerless before the breath of love.

We were not meant for ordinary passions,
In dull, correct, accommodating days.
We have the blaze of elemental forces
Burning in lips and hearts and words and eyes.

Our fast, volcanic love has long beginnings
In minstrels' ballads centuries ago.
And now it shakes us, presses on our hearts,
As, meekly, gratefully, we smile to feel
Its constant flight through ecstasy.

He'd sent it to Janet, or rather, to Shylle, who'd said it was beautiful. She found it more romantic than a proposal and, from then on, the two old people were regenerated night after night. Their fantasies took them further and further from their context and they lived the lives of the younger selves they still carried within them. One night, with the wind screeching outside William's cottage and the rain snare-drumming on Janet's windows in Skye, they were losing themselves as usual in Jason and Shylle.

'You know,' said Shylle, 'you and I must come from the only planet that lets their young go exploring without adult supervision'.

William bent closer to the screen to look at her. She was lying on her back on her black towel, the one with the vampire fangs etched in scarlet. Her skin smooth and delicious against the black of the towel and the white of the sand. She'd taken off her usual silver shimmer and left just two flimsy pieces of black material over her – one a thong which barely concealed her pubic mound, the other the half-mask she'd taken to wearing everywhere. It was a simple black strip, with no eye-holes. Rather than concealing her identity as masks are supposed to do, it hid the world from her.

'And what are we?' asked Jason. 'Young or adults?'

'That's the beauty of this,' said Shylle. 'Neither of us knows. We're old enough to open accounts and pay money and things, but then we launch ourselves here and we can splash in puddles, build sandcastles …'

'Or make glorious love,' said Jason, obeying the lusts which William never failed to suppress entirely.

'Hmmm. Yes, if we're really childish,' said Shylle.

Jason smiled.

'If we were on a real beach,' he said, 'we'd be sweating and the wind would be blowing this sand everywhere'.

'And instead of that,' she said, 'it simply wafts its warm air through our brains and blows gaps in our thoughts. And they float along on it, none of them connecting with the others.'

Despite Jason's coarse reversion to type in his too frequent allusions to making love, and the lusciousness of the body lying beside him, it was her strange flights of fancy that really drew him to her. She was exciting not because of the curves of her breasts and thighs, the fullness of her lips, the spill of autumn hair across the towel, but because her mind knew no limits. Others found that their avatars freed them from life's limitations and yet their only use of the freedom was to tread predictable paths. But she exulted in the simple fact that being an avatar meant that she didn't need to see at all. Being let loose in a world where, once they'd found the way out of the confusions of being a newcomer, almost everyone elected to be beautiful, fall in love, become tycoons, warlords or porn kings and queens, she chose instead the darkness, the unseen movements and stirrings of her dreams, etched briefly now and then in floating glints of light and deeper waves of shadow.

'Are you scared of the dark?' he asked.

She laughed – a real laugh. William's words were obviously very funny to her.

'Strange question,' she said. 'What's to be scared of? Darkness is where I am. It's fun, family, friends, and it's me – alone. The only other things there are the things I create.'

'Your vampires,' he said, thinking of the pictures on her walls.

She smiled that beautiful, illuminating smile.

'Vampires are simply happenings,' she said. 'Points at which the blackness thickens. Darkness connects everything, holds it all together. It doesn't pretend. Look at the lies scattered over this beach, the avatars, the pretences of eternity, the implications that sunshades and ice creams are significant. I prefer my black, personal infinity.'

William looked again at the mystery and magic of her shape against the towel and wondered what her eyes were seeing behind the black mask.

'Anyway,' she said, 'it's the only place we can have these conversations of ours.'

Jason lay back and William felt the heat of the sun and her body close beside him.

9 THE GODDESS CALIRA

A little further along the beach, an entirely different scenario was being played out. Jeremy Coulson, or Jeb, as his few friends called him, was as unreconstructed as they come. Amongst William's list-makers, he'd be the ring-leader. When he'd found AD, it was as if he'd stumbled into Wonderland. He couldn't believe it and, from the moment he glimpsed his first female avatar he was hooked. Jeb loved women – well, 'loved' wasn't the right word. He had no desire to be in any sort of permanent relationship with one, but he needed them in his life. Not to talk to or be friends with, of course. That was what guys were for. But women, with their breasts and curves and eyes and hair, they were essential. And in AD they were gorgeous, and they showed it and paraded around with cleavage spilling out and skirts up around their butts. It was paradise.

For Jeb, there was no real separation between AD and ND. He called his avatar Jeb, gave him all the same appetites and took every opportunity to indulge and satisfy them. He wasn't into all the Gorean stuff but he liked wandering around their towns and villages because there were so many beautiful slaves, kneeling around naked, some of them with profiles saying he could do more or less do what he liked with them, as long as he checked first with their master. And there were the clubs, the naked beaches, the porn enclosures. And some of the women were worse than men. They'd actually asked him if he wanted a fuck. His reply never varied. 'Do bears shit?' he said. (He knew that there was an expression something like that which was a cool way of saying yes.)

All of which meant that he racked up a very impressive total of fucks. Each night, he'd come home from work, phone for a pizza or bang something in the microwave, and settle down for some serious sex. He had so many women that, in the end, he'd created a special folder with sub-folders for the various categories. The main one was called 'FUCKS'. When he double clicked on it, as well as the more conventional 'BLONDES, BRUNETTES, REDHEADS, BALD, there were AMPUTEES, CONTORTIONISTS, FAIRIES, LESBIANS, MERMAIDS, NURSES, VAMPIRES and ZOMBIES.

Under each sub-heading except one, the names were in double figures. The only exception was LESBIANS, which contained one hundred and thirty-seven. Needless to say, this did not strike Jeb as anomalous. (Not that he knew the word, anyway.)

An extract from his conversation folder gives a flavour of the nature of these exchanges. One night, after three Asians, a Bald Athlete, and thirteen Lesbians, he wandered into one of his favourite spots – a store which sold action hooks. Near one of the corners, he saw a mermaid looking at a pair of hooks called 'Standing Room Only'. He went up to her and this is the conversation that followed:

JEB: Wanna try them?

MERMAID: What?

JEB: The hooks. Wanna fuck?

MERMAID: No.

JEB: Why not?

MERMAID: Well, the name of them.

JEB: So?

MERMAID: I've got no legs.

JEB: What d'you need legs for? We'll be lying down.

MERMAID: OK.

As you can see, romance was a foreign country for Jeb. Occasionally, a woman would try to intensify the experience by describing in relatively poetic terms the various anatomical changes she was feeling in herself or seeing on him, but Jeb's vocabulary was limited to a couple of synonyms for 'fuck' and he'd just mute her until they'd finished.

Then, on the beach a few metres along from Jason and Shylle, he met Calira.

Calira had achieved the impossible. In a virtual world full of beautiful, sexy women with flawless complexions, lovely faces and perfect figures, she surpassed everyone. She'd found a hair colour that carried tints of both spring and autumn, highlighted by the gold of a sunset. Her dark, dark eyes were flecked with silver, her half-parted lips shone plum-red and full, and the curves and proportions of her breasts, stomach, hips and thighs had rhythms and a perfection that were indescribable. Jeb saw her lying on the beach, her skin like pale chocolate against a dazzling white towel. For a while, he just looked, because even he knew that he would have to produce something special to get her attention and 'Wanna fuck?' was not the answer. But that, with variations, was all he had and, if he didn't move soon, some smart-assed guy would come along and start chatting with her.

He sat down, hesitated a while, then said, 'Nice day'.

Calira looked at him and smiled.

'Yes,' she said.

Jeb nodded and looked out to sea. So far, so good.

'Hot,' he said.

'Yes, it is.'

'No, not the weather. I meant you.'

'I don't understand,' said Calira.

'You're hot,' said Jeb.

'Yes,' said Calira. 'It's the sun.'

'No. Hot – like sexy.'

'Ah, I see. You mean I look suitable for carnal congress.'

'What?'

'Others have said the same thing to me. Not in quite the same way, but in essence they were conveying the fact that they found me attractive and wished to practise intercourse in one form or another.'

Jeb lifted his mirrored shades and looked at her.

'What did you say?' he asked.

'I said "Others have said the same thing to me. Not in ..."'

'No,' said Jeb. 'I mean what did you say when they asked you for a fuck?'

'It depended on the circumstances. Sometimes I told them I considered the act of penetration to be a form of violation, an invasion of an inner sanctum which should be the preserve only of the higher priests.'

'You fuck priests? Cool.'

'No. I was speaking metaphorically. I've often thought, jokingly, of the linguistic relationship between 'hole' and 'holy'.'

She slid her hand down across her stomach and cupped it around the little mound between her legs.

'Here,' she said, 'down deep, this ... entrance. In many ways it's a shrine, a secret place. For so many men, and women too, it's a Holy

Grail. They spend their lives seeking it, yearning for the completeness it will bring to them.'

She moved the other hand up to her breast, curling the fingers lazily beneath it. Sitting at his computer, Jeb was sweating and breathing hard. Usually, it took two or three minutes on one of the more energetic action hooks to achieve that.

Calira continued, the characters appearing slowly, lingeringly on the screen.

'They begin their journeys at my lips and breasts, using fingertips, lips and tongues to find their way to me, to try to tease from me the route their pilgrimage needs to follow.'

She lifted her lower hand gently then patted it back down.

'And this is always their goal. This mysterious valley, the tiny hillock at its head, the holy cavern lying deep in its interior.'

'Fuck me!' said Jeb.

It was an exclamation, not a request. Nonetheless, Calira chose to answer it.

'I'd have to consider that carefully,' she said. 'I can tolerate religion but not fanaticism. It all depends on the route you might take to that dark interior.'

'What? Where?' said Jeb.

His breathing was faster.

'I prefer acolytes to move softly to the entrance, with reverence and respect. They should begin to pay their homages with soft touches and softer words, dwelling on the threshold, taking time to prepare themselves for what lies beyond.'

Jeb only half knew what she was talking about, but her moving hands and his own breathlessness began to stir pulses in him.

'And, if I do allow them access to the entrance, they must be worthy of the sacredness of what they will discover in its interior,' said Calira. 'They must be strong enough to ride the torrents within, scale the smooth walls, reach for the central truth. They must release the Gods for me.'

'OK, OK,' said Jeb. 'Can I try?'

'Talk to me,' said Calira. 'Tell me of your journey, describe for me the vistas that open in your mind as you pass through the gates of my mystery into the moist and misty altars of our mutual deities.'

'OK, OK. Don't move, right?' said Jeb. 'I'll be back as soon as I can.'

He logged off, switched off his computer, and phoned his pal, Daryn.

'Hey, Dazza,' he said. 'I need some help. Wikipedia, a library, anything.'

In a small bedsit in Newcastle, Professor David Herrison leaned back in his wheelchair. He didn't imagine that anyone as monosyllabic as this Jeb character would provide anything of value to his research project on affective linguistic variables, but on his screen, Calira, his avatar, lay back on her towel and waited.

10 DESCARTES AND THE RABBIT

The trauma of losing control of Red stayed with Joe. The absurdity of assuming anyone could link abstractions, thinking, freedom with some form of concrete realisation of them was obvious. On the other hand, by creating AD, he'd done something very close to that. Joe remained a romantic, unwilling to reject the possibility of transcendence. And yet Red's exploitation of the gullibility of the FUCCers and the ease with which he'd turned their spiritual yearnings into a crazy articulation of flailing legs stressed the vast distances there were between the world of pixels and that of people. Nonetheless, Joe's pursuit of the elusive synthesis continued and, on more than one occasion, he felt certain he'd found it. That time, for example, he sent Ross to the underwater caves off the coast of Chile.

Ross was talking about Descartes. That wasn't unusual, it was the sort of pretentious stuff Joe had found himself doing more and more in AD. This time, though, it was slightly different. He was talking to a purple rabbit. Quite a tall one. Again, there's nothing remarkable about that, not in AD. But this was one of those furry things that disconcerted him. She had the Bugs Bunny face and ears, but a near perfect figure: 36D breasts (he was pretty confident the size was right; he'd become an expert on avatars), slim waist, and a 'two synchronised ferrets in a sack' butt. He was getting enthusiastic about the 'cogito' bit of the Descartes and a bit concerned that, by the time he got to the 'sum' bit, his gesticulating hands might inadvertently clutch a furry lump of mammary gland and, in the process, undermine his whole thesis.

They were standing on the pebbles of an underwater cave. Breathing without difficulty as the tropical fish swam around them and two couples from Denmark and Holland got more and more enthusiastic about the sets of action hooks strewn among the rocks there.

The rabbit seemed unaware of them.

'It's the "I" in "I think" that's the problem,' she said.

Joe knew that. Everybody knows that. But this was a pedantic rabbit. She needed to spell everything out. Joe decided to try to disorientate her.

'Kant,' he said.

Her hesitation was brief.

'Not only the name of the writer of the "Critique of Pure Reason"', she said. 'An apt description of its hypothesis, too. And,' she added, 'just a vowel away from encapsulating the man himself.'

One of the Danes stood up, a blonde, bronzed individual with ludicrous shoulders. A line of (Danish) chat splashed across the screen, followed by lol. Joe thought it was probably a Danish joke about sex.

A dachshund appeared from behind a clump of seaweed.

'Nice put-down, Doris,' it said to the rabbit.

That puzzled Joe. Her name tag identified her as Drindle Pinkneery.

'Doris?' said Ross.

'Yes?' said the rabbit.

'No, I mean – why did he call you Doris?'

'LOL. That's my real name. Dennis is my husband.'

'Dennis?' said Ross.

'Yes?' said the dachshund.

The Dane settled back into the action hook athletics. Joe looked at Ross. Young, dark hair, good looking. Not for the first time, the experience of virtuality disorientated him. He was, after all, a highly respected IT designer, with his own major company and millions in the bank. Why was he here on the sea bed talking about the nature of existence with a purple rabbit and a dachshund? He sighed; it was a question he seemed to be asking himself almost daily.

'Wet here,' said Dennis.

'It's symbolic,' said Doris.

'Of what?' asked Ross, immediately regretting prolonging his stay with them.

'All sorts of things,' she went on. 'The womb, lubrication, rain.'

'Wetness isn't a symbol of rain,' said Ross. 'It's a characteristic of it.'

'Alright, just the womb then,' said Doris.

'Dominicans,' said Dennis.

'What?' said Ross. (Joe was beginning to feel as if he was being subjected to some sort of brainwashing.)

'Founded in 1214,' said Dennis. 'Preached the gospel, fought against heresy. Great intellectual tradition, bags of philosophers.'

'And the connection with the womb? Or wetness?' said Joe, trying to make the words look sarcastic on the screen.

'Ah,' said Dennis, tapping the side of his nose with a paw.

Doris laughed.

'Dennis,' she said, 'stop teasing him.'

'Well, he should have realised by now,' said Dennis.

'Realised what?' said Ross/Joe.

'You think, therefore you are,' he said.

'So?'

'Who are you?'

'Ross Magee. Check the name tag.'

Dennis shook his head. Briefly, Joe admired the animation. So realistic. He allowed himself a small grin of pride.

'That's just a tag,' said Dennis. 'I asked who you "are" – from "to be". What's your essence?'

'What's yours?' replied Ross.

'I have none. I'm a dachshund,' said Dennis.

Joe thought that, for a dachshund, he was a smug bastard.

Suddenly, Ross was being hugged by Doris. Her furry arms were around him, her huge hairy breasts were crushing into his rib cage.

'Let's get back to wetness,' she said.

Joe was taken by surprise.

'Only if you take your head off,' said Ross, as Joe warmed to the idea of the breasts, convincing himself that Ross wasn't feeling rabbit mammaries against his chest, but a thick woollen bikini top.

'But that's where my cogito happens,' said the rabbit. 'Without my head, I don't exist, can't exist. Without that, no wetness.'

Suddenly, it hit Joe. She was right. This tall, purple rabbit was right. Here was Ross, sharing (on Joe's behalf) a womb with two Danes, a Dutch couple, a rabbit and a dachshund. They were all breathing under water. Impossible elements. Chaos, mayhem. All held together by the power of thinking, the willingness to believe that we can live our dreams. In his study back home, Joe spun round in his chair and looked out over Hampstead Heath. The Cartesian duality was a myth. The Frenchman said the body was a machine but the soul couldn't be defined by the laws of physics and yet the two acted on one another. Well, here and now, if Ross played his cards right (and somehow got rid of the dachshund), he could make this rabbit pregnant. Descartes didn't think of that when he was writing his Discourse on the Method. Joe was back in control.

11 GIRLS AND BOYS

It was the beginning of quite a settled period in the evolution of AD. By now, it was such a familiar part of the lives of people all over the world that its magic almost seemed 'normal'. Men strutted around in their everyday lives as if they really were as handsome and tireless as their AD avatars, women carried the power of their online adventures into their real homes and jobs and knew secretly that they were far more than the predictable creatures their husbands and partners seemed to make of them. The links between the two worlds were subtle but distinctly energising. The evidence of this egregious 'normality' was everywhere.

For example, if any of Sammy Preddle's real friends had known that he spent most of his evenings n AD, they would have found it hard to believe. In fact, 'friends' isn't quite the right word, because he wasn't close to anyone. There were people he worked with, people who lived in the same apartment block, two ex girl friends who were now married with kids but who sent him emails from time to time, and that was it.

Sammy lived a literal life. Perhaps it was a result of having a mathematical mind. For anyone with imagination, the world of maths was potentially a wondrous place. It implied an ability to handle pure concepts, unrelated to specific objects or images – undiluted thoughts that didn't even need words to articulate them, the mysterious music of equations and proofs. If that were the case with Sammy, the effect was to seal him in his thinking and keep his dreams and ambitions (if he had any) hidden from the outside world. He lived a life of compartments – always punctual at work, reading the same newspaper every day, watching the same tv programmes, drinking the same wine. The temptation was to assume that he suffered from some obsessive-compulsive disorder, but that would be a mistake. OCD sufferers have profound anxieties and an absolute need to follow specific rituals to maintain an equilibrium. Sammy had no such anxieties and his routines encompassed everything about him. In fact, his life was one gigantic ritual – everything in its place, ordered, secure and ... well ... normal.

In AD, his transformation was comprehensive. He'd first logged on because he read an article about it in his paper which concentrated on its technical aspects. The complexities of its social systems, the individual freedoms it unleashed, the insights into the human condition it afforded – none of these compared with the algorithms which formed its architecture. His avatar, Sami (so-called because 'Sammy' and other versions of the name were unavailable), wasn't a passport into a world of self-indulgence; it was simply mathematics in action. Sammy used it to test the algorithms which created it. But he was the only one who knew that. To all the people on his friends' list, Sami was a daredevil. He'd tried everything, from the simplest to the most extreme activities on offer. He'd visited all the research sites, taken the psychological tests, endured stressful situations, had pornographic couplings with women, men, animals and other avatars which fell into no recognisable categories (but which Sammy labelled 'pseudomorphs'). For a person with no imagination, he made astonishingly wide use of the resources of his virtual world.

Then, true to form, the time came for his summer holiday. He arrived home on the Friday evening, ate his meal (smoked fish with creamed potatoes and peas, as usual), and logged on. Holiday meant a change in routines. The fact that the avatar had done just about everything that could be done in AD was irrelevant. Every night, his activities had been the opposite of the tedium of Sammy's days in the office, so now that Sammy was on holiday, Sami would have to go to work.

Sammy searched the AD world for an office building with rooms to rent, visited several and eventually chose one in a busy location, full of malls, publishers, real estate agents and insurance offices. The room was on the third floor, accessible by translocation but also by a working lift. It had a desk, a filing cabinet, two easy chairs and some shelving. The rent was 500 virdollars a week. Sammy booked it for two weeks, then translocated Sami over, sent him up in the lift and sat him at the chair behind the desk.

And that's where he spent his summer holiday. Every morning for the following two weeks, Sammy got up, logged on, and sent Sami to the office. He'd watch him all day, occasionally walking him to the filing cabinet and back to the chair, until 5.30, when he'd translocate him back to his apartment and log off. In the evenings, Sammy would watch tv. His thoughts never strayed to Sami or AD. He was on holiday, so was Sami. The balance between his two lives was preserved. Once again, AD was serving its purpose. If Sammy had known any poetry (which he didn't), he would have appreciated the comfort and certainty offered by Robert Browning in *Pippa Passes*: 'God's in His Heaven, All's Right With the World'.

* * *

For Anna Barnes-Willoughby, on the other hand, what drew her to AD was its potential for excitement. The moment she heard about it, she knew that she had to try it. In life, she'd followed, almost religiously, the career trajectory that her parents, teachers and community had sketched out for her. She'd never yet taken a drug other than alcohol and even then, her use of it had been discreet, sparing and always correct. She lived in a detached, four-bedroomed house in Surrey. Her husband, a lawyer with a major bank, worked long hours, and her son and daughter were at a private school and only came home at weekends, so she had lots of spare time during the day.

Lunches with friends, hair appointments, shopping and cooking and, of course, her Pilates classes filled some of the hours but the creative urge that she'd been suppressing since her late teens continued to grow and become more urgent.

'You mean you get to make and dress your own ... what did you call it? ... avatar?' she said to Helen, who'd told her about these new virtual worlds.

'Yes,' said Helen. 'Mine's a nun.'

'Oh, that's so sweet,' said Anna, although she was surprised at the revelation since there was much talk at their Readers' Group of Helen's many extra-marital affairs.

Helen laughed.

'Not really,' she said. 'It keeps most of the men away, so I can choose the ones I want to spend time with. The minute I find one, my habits come off and I'm in skin-tight pink lycra which shows everything.'

'Helen,' said Anna, both shocked and excited by her words.

'But that's the point,' said Helen. 'You can be like that there. Anything goes. I've had better sex there than I've ever had with Don.'

Don was her husband, the non-executive director of six engineering companies and a well-known local rugby player. Anna found him loud, rude and generally unpleasant. But then, all men seemed perverse to her – wrapped up in their own worlds, incapable of understanding the delicacies and refinements that life could offer.

They talked some more about Helen's experiences as a nun, but Anna was eager to get home and try this wonderland for herself. She made an excuse about having an appointment with her manicurist, then drove home, checked that the phone was in answer mode, and settled at the computer.

The moment she was asked whether she wanted her avatar to be male or female and was presented with a standard, characterless female form, her mind leapt over thirty years back into her past and she was with her first Barbie doll again. She'd been crazy about them. She bought them in all their forms, had boxes full of outfits, herds of ponies, and the pink carriages to go with them, houses, furniture, tea-sets, ball gowns, jodhpurs, swimsuits; Anna was the archetypal Barbie girl.

And now, once more, she was being given the chance to slough off the cares of being a respectable wife, mother and member of a fine middle class community, and play with dolls.

She noticed other avatars, male and female, coming and going around her but, for days and days, she ignored them all and lost herself in refining her avatar's appearance, buying clothes and accessories and animations that let her walk and pose like the stars she admired so much in 'Hello' magazine. The fact that Beebie (her avatar) could do such things made her so much more satisfying than dear Barbie had ever been. Anna could launch her creation onto dance floors, into beach parties, shops and clubs and she looked like and was much closer to a real person than Barbie could ever be.

It was the fulfilment of a dream. Inside the woman who'd become a wife and mother, the girl who'd dreamed with her dolls still existed, as full of fancies as ever, and convinced that this was a world in which the transcendence she craved would be possible.

To begin with she WAS Barbie – or rather, Beebie. In the same way that she saw other residents BEING their dreams – cats, dogs, teddy bears, dragons – it was so wonderful. All these people had rediscovered a childhood passion and were free to revisit it and indulge themselves in developing it further – sometimes to astonishing extremes.

One day, after she'd groomed her pony, taken her shower and was looking through the 'Wardrobe' box in her personal files to decide what to wear, the thought of Ken crept into her mind once more. It had happened before but the idea that, with the magic available in this world, a relationship with Ken could go so much further than it ever had in reality, had caused her to shake the thought from her mind.

She was used to sitting stiff-legged Kens and Barbies at picnic tables or in the dining rooms of plastic mansions, holding tiny cups and glasses to their lips. The thought that Beebie might actually be embraced by a Ken equivalent was at first unseemly; she was the embodiment of purity, a perpetual virgin. Even when her brother had crucified one of her Kens on the trunk of a cherry tree when she was nine, the realities of the harsh world in which they lived had still not sullied her dreams.

But now, her living Barbie could … make love. The temptation was strong but Anna quickly rationalised it, decided that it was, after all, only virtual experiences she'd have, and they couldn't impact on her real marriage. And she began planning how she might find someone worthy of Beebie.

It went without saying that his name had to be Ken. She typed it into the search facility and was delighted, if rather taken aback, to discover that there were over a hundred. Now that she'd decided on this course of action, she was too eager to progress with it to bother reading all their details, so she selected some at random and, in the end, chose one who hadn't bothered to write anything at all. Her decision was based solely on the fact that he'd joined on the same day that she had. After several deep breaths and a secret smile at how fast her heart was beating, she sent him a personal message.

She'd thought he wouldn't be there, so she was surprised to get an answer right away. With no time to work out a strategy, she dashed off something close to the truth – her Barbie craze, the attraction of his name, the fact that she hadn't yet made many friends because she'd been too busy getting Beebie just right – and she was thrilled when he seemed to understand her and suggest that he'd been using AD in exactly the same way.

In the end he suggested they should meet and Anna, more and more excited that Beebie would be getting together with her Ken, agreed, saying only that they should leave it until the following day, to give her time to think through what she wanted and what they might do. Ken gave her a location marker for a street in Paris near the Eiffel Tower and they said their goodbyes.

That night, after a meal of roast chicken with green beans and garlic, she allowed her husband to have the usual perfunctory sex then lay unable to sleep. The next day was endless as she crawled slowly towards the time of Beebie's appointment with Ken. At last, she logged on and tried on outfit after outfit as she waited for three o'clock to arrive. The second it did, she typed in the location co-ordinates and sat back as Beebie flashed and sparkled her way through the skies to the rendez-vous.

She looked around. Yes, there was the Eiffel Tower, and the streets were lined with boutiques and cafes with tables on the pavements outside them. But there were no other people yet. Her street was empty save for a blue, low-slung Corvette coupé. She turned through 360 degrees just to check, and it was only when she fixed on the car again that she noticed the number plate: KEN 1. She smiled and moved towards it.

'Hi,' said Ken, without getting out. 'God, you're gorgeous.'

The passenger door of the car swung open and Beebie stooped to get in. Then Anna paused. There was no driver.

'Where are you?' said Beebie.

'LOL,' said Ken. 'I'm here. You're climbing into me.'

Beebie stood and stepped back.

'I told you,' said Ken. 'I've spent as much time on my avatar as you have on yours. I'm a 430 horse power, 6.2 litre LS3, with a V8 aluminium-block engine, short-throw six-speed manual transmission, and split-spoke silver-painted aluminium wheels.'

'You're a car,' said Anna.

'Of course I'm a car,' said Ken. 'But if you don't like this avatar, I've got others.'

Anna was relieved, then Ken went on.

'I've got a 6 cylinder, 245 hp Porsche Boxster with 273 Nm maximum torque at 4,600 - 6,000 rpm and a compression ratio of 11.0:1. There's also a 4.2 litre Jaguar XK Convertible, a Toyota Avensis with sequential automatic transmission, a flat four overhead valve 1486 cc Jowett Javelin with twin Zenith carburettors ...'

As his words continued to jump onto the screen, Anna turned Beebie round and began to walk her away down the boulevard. Beebie's hips swung with the same exotic insolence, but Anna was ready to cry. Why were men always such a disappointment? She sat back in her chair as Beebie continued her stroll and Ken's words still trailed across the screen.

'OK, HOW ABOUT A CITROEN DS WITH A PRESSURISED NITROGEN SUSPENSION SPHERE AND BUTTERFLY VALVE CARBURETTOR?'

12 SETTLING DOWN

It had been a chastening experience for Anna, but the magic of the Barbie-Ken story never fades, and she quickly convinced herself that her car-Ken had been an aberration. This time, when she called up the list of Kens again, she made sure she read the information they'd given about themselves – either as avatars or in their normal lives. When she read that one Ken was, in fact, Karl Andersson, a forty-two year old geologist in Iceland, who liked reading, cycling, hill walking, log fires and sunsets, she felt a stirring of interest, especially as he was also unmarried. The details he hadn't given were that he still lived with his mother, he'd had girl friends but was too shy to risk commitment or even to get much beyond kissing them, and that AD was his preferred reality.

He turned out to be a regular male avatar without the pushiness of most and Anna was so sweet and gentle in her dealings with him that he even agreed to reshape his avatar to resemble the original Ken, (with shorter hair and no stupid grin). They built a house together, bought clothes, furniture, even a car (which Ken let her choose). For Karl, the interest shown by Anna was a totally new experience and he was determined not to hold back. He bought so many action hooks – for eating breakfast together, gardening, cooking, dancing and even kissing quite passionately – that he began to take an interest in the programs which produced the animations. His research was purposeful as he accessed the instructions, pulled them apart and saw how the movements were captured and regenerated in the computer. In the end, he thought 'I can do this'.

His idea was to create hooks which would help him to mark the special nature of his relationship with Anna/Beebie by taking it into areas not available to others. There were already almost unlimited actions couples could perform, from the most innocent through progressively more frantic sexual variations to scarcely imaginable perversions. But Karl's dreams were nothing like as extravagant. He sought instead the unique comforts that came with gentle domestic routines, the very things that were missing from the existence of a virgin approaching middle age who still lived with his mum.

Gradually, he introduced Beebie to evenings spent toasting marshmallows, sitting almost motionless watching TV with only the occasional glance and smile passing between them as they enjoyed the programmes, or washing up together in total silence. Whenever he clicked on his 'mowing the lawn' hook, Beebie would automatically stand up, get out the ironing board and start pressing shirts. If he sent her shopping, his own avatar would go with her and stand around in the shops fidgeting and looking at his watch more and more frequently. For Karl, the comforting automatism of an intensely normal couple was highly satisfying.

Anna, on the other hand, soon tired of it. At first, the fact that Beebie and Ken were so demonstrably a couple was cute. They really were doing the things she'd done with her own Ken and Barbie way back. But the silences became oppressive and the distance between Beebie and Ken began to grow.

'This is fine, honey,' Beebie said to Ken one day. 'But it's not going anywhere.'

'Where would you want it to go?' asked Ken.

Beebie had no answer.

'I don't know, but it's too calm, too perfect. We need something to remind us just how perfect it is.'

This didn't make much sense to Karl. Anna tried explaining it to him.

'You're so sweet, we belong together, but it's all on the one level.'

'It's a level I love, my darling,' said Karl.

'I know, sweetie, but … but … well, think of how nice it'd be if we ever had to make up.'

'What d'you mean?'

'Well, if we had a quarrel …'

Ken laughed. Beebie went on.

'... No, really. Just a tiny spat. Then we'd feel sad at the rift, we'd want to be back to where we were again, and the making up would be so sweet.'

Karl still didn't understand, but the fear of losing Anna's love set him thinking.

Over the next few days, Anna occasionally saw that Karl was online but, apart from walking in, giving Beebie a quick kiss on the cheek, then leaving again, Ken made little attempt at contact. He spent all the time in his shed in the garden. She began to wonder whether Karl had misunderstood her and was drawing back.

She got her answer eight days after the original conversation about making up. Beebie was sitting in the lounge, flicking through a fashion magazine when Ken walked in, kissed her on the cheek and set two action hooks, just labelled 'him' and 'her' on the coffee table.

'What's this, honey?' Beebie asked.

'A surprise, baby,' said Ken.

'Oh you're such a tease. Give me a clue. Pleeeeaaase.' The last word was drawn out on the screen, making it into the equivalent of a babyish pout.

Ken smiled then Karl clicked on the hooks. They both disappeared – the 'him' into Ken and, simultaneously, the 'her' into Beebie.

'Oh, for Christ's sake, stop being such a fucking baby,' said Ken.

To Anna's amazement, Beebie threw the magazine down, stood up and yelled 'Me? What about you, asshole? Bringing even more shit into the house and expecting me to be impressed. Loser.'

'Yeah, I feel like a loser, stuck with a frigid bitch like you,' yelled Ken.

In Surrey, Anna felt the heat in her blushing cheeks. She'd never said such things before, and even though Beebie was pacing about saying them now, they were nothing to do with Anna. In Reykjavík, however, Karl had a broad grin on his face and his mother called up to ask what he was laughing at.

'Nothing, mother,' he called back as he watched Ken grab Beebie by the arms and hold her so that he was staring straight into her eyes, their faces inches apart.

'Day after day I sit here listening to the shit you speak,' he snarled. 'Crap about dresses, broken nails, the wrong coloured lipsticks. Shit, shit and more shit. You make me puke.'

Beebie tried unsuccessfully to break free.

'Let me go, you bastard,' she screamed. 'If you weren't such a pathetic asshole we'd be doing more interesting things, living a little, instead of being stuck in this shitty house.'

'When have you ever done anything interesting?' said Ken, shaking her. 'You're just a fucking clothes horse, an empty-headed bimbo with tits for brains.'

'Huh, any brains you ever had disappeared the minute your balls dropped,' yelled Beebie.

And so it went on, their insults getting richer and richer as the program Karl had written chose from the extensive list he'd sourced from the *Mammoth Book of Domestic Repartee*. There were some silences as Ken stared out of the window and Beebie dabbed her eyes with a hankie but mostly, they yelled about each other's inadequacies, irritating personal habits, sexual shortcomings and dubious parentage. Anna learned words she'd never heard or seen before and Karl's English got better and better, although he'd need to be careful to choose the contexts in which he could use the new vocabulary.

At last, he pulled his keyboard towards him and typed 'Oh darling. I'm so sorry. Forgive me.'

Nothing happened. The only words that appeared on the screen came from Beebie.

'You couldn't satisfy a mouse with what you've got.'

'Huh, its bloody droppings would have more sex appeal than you do,' shouted Ken.

Karl smiled but nonetheless felt a little anxiety. He'd forgotten to override the program before trying to repossess Ken. He pulled down the general AD menu and clicked on 'animation override' before starting to type again.

'Oh baby, I'm so, so sorry,' he wrote.

'Fuck off, dickhead,' yelled Beebie.

'Bull dyke bitch,' shouted Ken.

Karl's anxiety grew. He clicked on the override again and again but the two avatars continued to circle one another and hurl obscenities. Then the horrible truth dawned. The override was designed for legitimate, in-house animations. His own didn't have the key they needed to engage with it. He'd just assumed they would and so he hadn't bothered to create hooks for the making up afterwards. Until he did, Ken and Beebie would continue this dance of mutual vilification.

He logged off and began working on the new programs, hoping they would have the power to counteract the highly effective quarrelling hooks. Each day he logged on and found Ken and Beebie still at it, tireless in their search for and discovery of new slurs and abuses. In order to test his making up efforts, he created two new avatars and set them quarrelling. He tried prototype after prototype on them and at last managed to design one powerful enough to make them stop and respond to his normal commands again. He tried it several times, then logged on and took the new hooks into the lounge.

He ignored the calls of 'Pygmy-dick' and 'Pustule' from Beebie and 'Rancid whore' and 'Shagnasty cow' from Ken, and clicked on the hooks. They vanished as before and an uncanny stillness fell.

Hesitatingly, he typed 'Darling?'

There was a long pause before Beebie's words appeared.

'What happened?' she said.

'I was stupid,' said Karl. 'Wrote a stupid program. I wanted a quick quarrel, then … well, like you said, to make up. But making up was hard to do.'

'Come here,' said Beebie.

Ken sat beside her on the couch. She curled herself up against him.

'Forgive me?' said Ken.

'Nothing to forgive,' said Beebie. 'It was a misunderstanding. We were both silly. Said things we didn't mean.'

'Yes. I never want another argument. I just want us to keep loving the way we do.'

'So do I, my darling,' said Beebie. 'But it was interesting, all the same. Exciting even.'

'Too exciting for me. I thought I'd lose you,' said Ken.

'Silly,' said Beebie.

They clung together, happy to be restored to normal. Eventually, it was Beebie who broke the silence. She nuzzled her lips nearer to Ken's ear and said, 'Fucking good argument, though, wasn't it?'

13 HEALTH AND SAFETY

When Joe Lorimer came across examples such as these, he felt reassured. People were using AD not just for extremes of experience but also to enrich their day to day lives, to learn to value the simple pleasures as well as the extremes. There was, however, one development in AD that irritated him more and more as he came across its impact on residents' lives. For all the omniscience of Red Loth and for all Joe's algorithmic skills, he was powerless before the activities of a group of residents who'd formed themselves into a Health and Safety Inspectorate.

The first he heard of them was when Ross Magee was helping a family build a log cabin in a clearing half way up a mountain in Canada. Building in AD has none of the stresses and dangers of its ND equivalent. The avatars simply produce a block of wood out of thin air then stretch it until it's the right size for the wall, door, ceiling, or whatever other function it'll serve. They lie another layer of patterning over it – wallpaper, logs, tiles and so on – and simply stick the pieces together. When the whole house is built, they can then stretch it further to fit their chosen plot or accommodate any extra family members who appear. It's a quick, satisfying process.

Ross was working on decorating the porch with hanging baskets of flowers when some words appeared on the screen.

'What d'you think you're doing?'

He looked around to find two men, one with a clipboard, the other with a briefcase. It was briefcase-man who'd spoken. He pointed at the porch and repeated the question.

'What d'you think you're doing?'

'What's it look like?' said Ross.

'A porch,' said the man.

His colleague wrote a note on the clipboard.

'Satisfied?' said Ross.

The man went to the porch, looked all round it, touched one basket and made it swing, then said, 'Not by a very long chalk. Got the dimensions of this?'

'Course not,' said Ross. 'It was about the size of a shoe box when I made it. I just expanded it until it fitted the doorway. Anyway, why're you asking that?'

'Needs to be at least thirty-seven centimetres higher than the tallest resident or potential guest.'

'Who said so?'

The man nodded at his colleague who held up his clipboard and showed him some paper headed 'HSI – Keeping you safe, not sorry'.

'Never heard of you,' said Ross.

'Headquarters are in Brussels but the legislation applies world-wide,' said the man.

'Says who?'

'Article 387, para. 12, sub-section 32a,' said the man.

He tapped the side of the porch.

'If you want this to stay here, you'll need to put up notices of its dimensions. You'll also need warnings that residents should resize their avatars before approaching within 3.479 metres of the threshold.'

'Wait a minute,' said Ross. 'How many avatars have banged their heads on porches?'

'Thanks to our regulations, none,' said the man.

'Crap,' said Ross. 'They don't need regulations. Even if they did bang into a porch, so what? It wouldn't hurt them.'

'That's not the point,' said the man. 'They could sue the owner. But not if his signage complied with regulations.'

'Listen,' said Ross. 'I know the guy who designed all this and his idea was to get rid of bloody regulations. He wanted individuals here to be free.'

'That's a common error in all forms of government,' said the man. 'Individual freedom of expression leads to anarchy – just look at the USA.'

'There's no anarchy there.'

'There would be if their lawyers weren't so conscientious.'

The man took a few paces towards Ross and stopped beside him.

'You see, societies need to be regulated,' he said. 'People need guidance. They like to know where they stand. There has to be an official line. Everything the HSI does is for the good of AD residents.'

'Like what?' asked Ross.

'Well, next month we'll be rolling out our "HFE" initiative.'

Ross just looked at him.

'Health For Everyone,' said the man. 'Avatars don't exercise nearly enough.'

'What?' said Ross. 'Why do they need to exercise?'

'If they don't, they'll get fat.'

'Avatars don't get fat. They're bunches of pixels,' said Ross.

The man looked at his colleague.

'Show him,' he said.

The colleague thumbed through some pages on his clipboard and held it up for Ross to see. He'd revealed a graph showing correlations between physical activity (or lack of it) and obesity. Underneath was the equation $p2(4p - \beta3)(\sin\pi \div \sqrt{4.65}) \approx \Omega10.3$.

'What the fuck's this?' said Ross.

'Quantifiable variables consistent with exponential progressions in a parallax matrix,' said the man.

'I'd never have guessed,' said Ross.

In the end, Joe left the two men with the house builders and logged off. He immediately looked through the central database to find out what he could about these HSI people. They'd begun as a small group in London and spread like a virus through the whole of AD, even sending missionaries to islands in the South Pacific, up the Amazon and into unexplored regions of Africa. People had joined in order to conform to their famous regulations and the movement had gained a momentum to match that of the Catholic Church.

If nothing else, Joe had to admire their commitment to their cause even though its consequences were disastrous. One of the regular major tourist attractions in AD was the quarterly migration of lemmings off various cliffs. Thousands of avatars used to gather to watch the Kamikaze spectacle. Then, one autumn, the HSI insisted that each individual lemming sign an affidavit attesting it was of sound mind and absolving the landowner of any responsibility for its upcoming fate. The forms were long and difficult to understand so instead of a progressively denser flood of fur pouring over the cliff and down into the sea, the spectacle was that of a clifftop crammed with perplexed, agitated lemmings scratching their heads and chewing their biros, with masses more waiting in queues for their turn, and only the occasional plop as an individual completed its form, got it countersigned and was given permission to leap.

The trade in hiring unicorns was badly hit, too, when the Inspectorate insisted that herds be tested regularly for equine ailments from Aural plaques and Bog Spavin to Urticaria and Windgalls. One summer, entire herds in lower Tuscany had to be destroyed when they were found to be suffering all the symptoms of Equine Infectious Anaemia – fever, body oedema and lethargy. In the worst cases, their horns actually started growing downwards into their skulls causing severe personality disorders.

There was the occasional example of an HSI campaign which produced desirable results. As in the case of Zinzan Dill, a research assistant in one of the private AD hospitals. Hospitals in AD are, of course, unnecessary but they do offer particularly rich avatars another way of displaying their wealth. Zinzan was awarded a grant to investigate the possibility of creating an animation that would, when triggered, produce a subtle blushing effect on an avatar's cheeks and neck. It was all part of the refinements that Joe had hoped would materialise as residents became more involved with AD's processes. The problem for Zinzan was that he was rather too enthusiastic.

When he launched his program at a gathering of the hospital's administrators, it was clear that he'd taken the effect a step too far. He used his own avatar as a guinea pig and, at first, the watching bureaucrats were impressed as they saw the pink wash rising up his neck and into his cheeks. Their approval was soon withdrawn, however, when his colour deepened, his hair started blushing, and blood began dripping from his nose. Within eight seconds, it was also gushing from his ears, eyes and mouth. Fortunately, an HSI member was on hand to halt the demonstration before news of the rogue experiment permeated through to any patients and thus prevented them becoming even richer by suing the hospital for failing to conduct adequate risk assessments.

As Joe logged out of the database, he reluctantly had to acknowledge that organisations such as the HSI were inevitable products of the normalisation of the AD experience. He couldn't imagine them having any success in dealing with Goths, vampires or any of the sprawling communities of fairies, elves, goblins, dragons and other sprites and monsters in AD, but for the ordinary, timid humanoids, men with clipboards were a sort of reassurance that the world still had form and purpose.

14 CATS

The clipboard fetishists preferred to live their safely guarded AD lives in ignorance of some of the extremes in its darkness. Not even the most fastidiously correct HSI inspector could have coped, for example, with what happened to Bob Gantleton. For his AD avatar, Milton Zork, he'd chosen a dark-eyed, dark-haired male in black leathers, but he could see the attraction of being a cat. At first, he hadn't understood why people wanted to do that when there was such a wide choice of human body shapes and sizes and so much variety in the features you could give yourself. He watched the feline avatars stand there with their ears twitching and their tails swishing from side to side and found his curiosity growing about the actual physical nature of the persons who'd chosen to represent themselves in that way. The more cats he'd met, the more fascinating they seemed to become. There was one in a pale tiger skin who wore bling necklaces and jewels and looked sensational. When she occasionally used one of her other avatars – a blue-eyed redhead with the statutory perfect figure – he felt less inclined to spend time with her.

It was Lucy who explained it all to him. She'd appeared on a dance floor once, weaving her own individual moves among the others, who were all coupled in the tangled intricacies of the samba or else glued together and swaying through one of the slower dances. At one point she'd bumped into Milton and apologised. Milton's partner, a Goth with red teardrops tattooed on both cheeks, had told her to fuck off and Lucy had stopped and said, 'My dear girl, I understand that your apparel expresses your desire to resist convention. Such resistance is always the refuge of those who are struggling with a sense of inadequacy. I've no doubt yours is very deep and I should feel sympathy for you instead of amused disdain, but telling me to fuck off provokes just one reaction. Shove it up your ass, sister.'

The Goth could only manage another 'Fuck off' and Lucy resumed her solitary gliding. But she did take the time to send Bob a personal message and, eventually, the two of them became close friends. Strangely, the Goth was somehow changed by the incident. She spent the rest of the evening complaining of a headache and pains in her neck and, just a week later, she failed to sign on at her usual time and Bob never saw her again.

Milton and Lucy were never lovers, always friends, and hung out together whenever they could. Bob was surprised to find that she liked the occasional visit to a BDSM site and was happy to send personal messages to him while she allowed herself to be strapped to various devices and ill-treated by more or less articulate masters. It was all part of what she called 'full-on living'. She craved sensations, was always looking for new experiences. As a human avatar she'd quickly exhausted the possibilities but launching herself as a cat forced her to think in different ways.

'You know,' she said, 'I think I even move like a cat in normal life nowadays. I'm more aware of my body, I can achieve an amazing stillness when I listen for something. My reactions have sharpened. Oh, and I don't need anyone. I'm totally self-reliant.'

'Weren't you like that before?' asked Bob.

'Nope,' she replied. 'Always needed reassurance, or at least confirmation that I was making the right choices. Not any more.'

'And you think that's come from being a cat?'

'No doubt about it.'

As the weeks and months went by, Bob heard more and more about Lucy's everyday life. Her real name was Beatrice and she lived alone in a smallish town in the foothills of the Alps. She'd had a husband but one year he went to Rio for Mardi Gras and never came back. She had no living relatives and earned money by proof-reading manuscripts for a publisher in London. Her days were spent at her computer and her only pastime, apart from wandering through various virtual worlds, was to take long walks or ride her chestnut pony in the hills after the sun had set.

Then she told him about Sukie.

Sukie was a kitten who'd just walked through her front door one day, three years before, and sat looking at her. She was tiny, with two white paws and a perfect diamond of white fur between her eyes. Beatrice had picked her up, she'd snuggled into her neck and Beatrice knew that she had to keep her.

Sukie cost her nothing. There was never any need to buy the expensive cat food that was so extravagantly praised in TV adverts as if it was a gastronomic marvel. Sukie always found her own food, coming back from forays into the fields and woods around the house with blood on her face and claws and jumping onto Lucy's lap to purr and lick herself clean.

'She's perfect. So self-sufficient,' said Beatrice. 'I could never be as … self-contained as she is. I know you think it's crazy but she and I understand one another.'

'Maybe not crazy,' said Bob, 'but I think you need to get out more, see some people.'

Beatrice laughed.

'Sukie wouldn't like that,' she said. 'Sometimes we get sales people coming to the door. She sits just inside watching me as I speak to them, and I can feel her disapproval. Once, I went for a test drive with a man who was delivering my new car and, when I got back, she jumped onto my lap, stood with her front paws on my chest and looked straight into my eyes.'

'Scary,' said Bob.

'Yes,' said Beatrice. 'But then she purred and lay against me with her head curled under my chin. But,' she added with a smile,' she did give me a little nip in the neck – just to show she disapproved.'

'What do you suppose she thinks about you talking to me like this then?' asked Bob, looking at Milton and Lucy sitting on the grass in a park.

'She's looking at you now,' said Beatrice. 'She always sits on my lap as I type. She watches the screen. I think she knows you.'

'Not sure I like that,' said Bob. 'She might put me in the same category as the car guy.'

'Oh no. I know what she's feeling. I don't think she minds you.'

'How about the guys at the BDSM places?'

'She watches. Looks at me now and then, then turns back to the screen. I think it … amuses her.'

'Bloody hell. A laughing cat … no, a laughing, sadistic cat,' said Bob.

Beatrice smiled.

Under a tree behind the two avatars Bob noticed two action hooks labelled 'Temptation'.

'I wonder what she'd think if we jumped on those hooks,' he said.

'She'd hate it,' said Beatrice.

'How come?' said Bob.

'I just know she would.'

'So it's funny if other guys carve lumps off Lucy and stick all sorts of bits of metal into her and up her, but not if poor old Milton there puts a friendly arm round you. That's weird.'

'Stop, Bob,' said Beatrice. 'She understands you.'

Bob laughed.

'Now I know you're taking the piss,' he said. 'You're saying she can read too.'

'Not read, no. But she knows. She and I are … very close. It's hard to explain. Hard to understand even. We're cats.'

'No, Beatrice. You're a woman. Your avatar is a cat. It seems to me that …'

He stopped. The circle of stars had appeared telling him she was offline and, moments later, Lucy had disappeared.

He thought little of it. She often got cut off – the weather up in the mountains did strange things with her connections and she was sometimes off for a day or more. But when a whole week went by without her reappearing, he was puzzled. They'd been meeting online for over a year and she'd always told him when she'd be going away for any length of time. Sometimes she had to go to London for meetings with the publisher and now and then she liked to go camping in the hills.

After three weeks he was genuinely concerned. If she'd decided to stop logging on, he knew she'd have told him. He searched online for newspapers published in her region, even finding her local evening paper. He read the obituaries and scanned the headlines for news of accidents or mishaps. But there was just silence. And yet he couldn't just forget about her. It seemed strange to log on knowing that she'd be missing from all their usual places.

Two months later, he still couldn't get her out of his head and he decided to try to find out what the hell had happened. He knew that she lived on the eastern fringes of her town, at the foot of a particular hill. He wrote to the town's police department, phrasing his letter very carefully and explaining that he was concerned for the safety of his friend and would appreciate news of her. Two weeks later, he received a reply. It thanked him for bringing their attention to the fact that Beatrice seemed to be missing and regretted to inform him that his friend was dead. They also said that they would be sending two of their officers to see him and they'd appreciate it if he would answer some questions about his relationship with her. Bob was stunned. What the hell could have happened? How was his relationship with her relevant?

He would find out in due course, but nothing he'd imagined would be close to what the police had found when, getting no replies to their knocking on Beatrice's door, they'd forced the lock and gone inside. The smell immediately told them what to expect, but not the full extent of it. In the dining room, the computer was sitting on the table, its screen still flickering, a chair in front of it. The table all round it was thick with dried blood, blood which had spilled onto the floor and all over the chair. On and around the chair were bones, rags of flesh and a woman's clothes. And, in the middle of it all sat a tiny kitten, with two white paws and a perfect diamond of white fur between her eyes.

15 THE PRINCESS

Extremes such as that which befell Beatrice were rare, but in a way, there were even worse stories – not stories of gore and horror, but stories of quiet despair. In the life of Rhona Pearl, for example, romance was an unknown word – and concept. She lived in a flat in a tenement building. It had four rooms: one bedroom for her, another for her two kids, a cupboard-sized bathroom and the fourth for everything else. Her husband had left her the previous July, when she told him of her second pregnancy and, since then, she'd hardly been outside the flat, except for necessary journeys to buy food and, in charity shops, clothes for the kids. In some ways, this was a bonus. It meant she didn't have to wear make-up or buy clothes for herself, which she couldn't afford anyway. While the kids were awake, she fed them, played and watched TV with them and sometimes looked out of the window at the rows of flats in the buildings across the street. But when she'd got them to bed and eaten a quick snack, she switched on the computer which her husband had left 'for the kids' and became a princess.

Because Rhona was also Angeldust Starshine, concubine of Tristan Malevolans, who was ruler of the entire Alternative Dimension enclosure of StormFront and commander of two battalions of Borgian Exterminators. She didn't know Tristan's real name. She knew he had lots of money because he'd bought his enclosure and even offered to buy one for her but, beyond that and the fact that he gave every impression of having an IQ in single figures, he was an enigma. In fact, he'd chosen the name Tristan because his real name was Stanley and Malevolans because he thought it sounded like a cool make of car – a Mazerati Malevolans maybe.

They'd met when he and a small patrol of Exterminators had marched into a ballroom by a moonlit lake. Their intention had been to rape and pillage but every time they tried to steal something, they couldn't because the 'Steal' level on their Acquire Column was greyed out and whenever they tried to rip the clothes off a woman, she translocated somewhere else. When they tried it on Rhona, she stood her ground and refused to sit on the rape action hooks they'd brought with them. Tristan had also been impressed and intrigued by her use of so many words with more than one syllable. They'd talked, he'd taken her back to StormFront and they'd made love in more ways than Tristan knew were possible, mainly because she knew so many polysyllabic synonyms for 'fuck'. Since then, she'd been his concubine. He didn't know what that meant except that it wasn't a wife and it sounded sexual.

But she'd been more to him than a good lay. Whenever he had meetings with other warlords, Rhona would keep Angeldust out of sight behind a curtain and prompt Tristan with personal messages. Apart from ensuring that his strategies and tactics were always on a par with those of his enemies, this also added an intriguing dimension to his character. At these meetings, with her guidance, he would unfold delicate strategies which, on the surface, looked straightforward but proved to be far more flexible than others had expected. Once, when Thor DagHald had admired a particular coup, Tristan sat back on his throne, read the secret messages Rhona sent him, then growled 'The psychology of despair has no evasive potential when disillusion is its counterpoint'.

Rhona had picked the words at random from an article in a newspaper which had been wrapped around a cabbage she'd bought from the corner shop. Thor nodded sagely and repeated the words to his own concubine when he got home that evening. But then, on the occasions when Rhona was away, Tristan's responses to questions were mainly confined to grunts or 'How the fuck would I know?' Since in Council meetings he seemed to be capable of such meticulous analysis of any situation or strategy, others would interpret these moods as signals that the evil deep within him was too near the surface, overwhelming his intellect, and that they should retire until he found his true voice again. In their eyes, thanks to Rhona, Tristan was simultaneously Beast and DemiGod.

On Tuesday, Rhona had had a hard day. Her eldest child, Donald, had been sick twice, once at the table and once in his bed. He was running a temperature and it was late before he eventually fell into a restless sleep. His retching had exhausted him, but he tossed and turned for ages before her version of The Dixie Chicks' 'Godspeed' lulled him into oblivion. Her nerves were frayed and she wondered whether she should just watch television, but she'd promised Tristan that she'd be there to help him prepare a speech which he had to give to the Borgian War Council so, with a sigh, she logged on and became Angeldust again.

'Where the fuck you been?' was Tristan's greeting.

'Sorry,' said Rhona. 'Trouble with the kids.'

'OK. Let's do it then.'

'Do what?'

'The fucking speech.'

'Oh, right. What's it supposed to be about?'

'I dunno. Hang on. They bunged me a note. Here it is.'

The note came up on Rhona's screen. It was called 'Territorial acquisition policy for the Fifth Quadrant'. She skimmed through the headings and saw quite quickly that it was yet another example of bullshit. One of the warlords on the Council was a university lecturer. He'd made sure everyone knew it and, whenever they wanted something to sound impressive, they asked him to write it down. This time, he'd provided the theoretical outlines for a successful invasion of the island of Balthazaria and the Council had asked Tristan to turn them into practical applications.

'OK,' said Rhona. 'So you're going to invade Balthazaria.'

'Are we?' said Tristan.

'Yes. It's an island, so how would you start?'

'Boats,' said Tristan.

Rhona skimmed down the headings.

'Right,' she said at last. ' That'll be "The logistical imperatives of marine mobility".'

She began expanding the heading and writing what to her were quite unnecessary arguments to say that, if anyone wanted to invade an island surrounded by water, they'd need boats. When she'd finished, she asked the next question.

'What about when you get there?'

'Kill 'em,' said Tristan.

'Not all of them,' said Rhona.

'Why not?'

'You'll need to set up a local administrative structure. If you try imposing an externally manned bureaucracy, you'll encourage terrorism and, at the very least, civil resistance.'

'Oh, fuck it,' said Tristan. 'Just write anything.'

'Cuddle me while I'm doing it,' said Rhona.

'Oh fuck, OK,' said Tristan.

He got up and stretched out on some cushions next to his throne. Rhona tucked Angeldust into his embrace, looked at his huge tattooed arms around her, felt how her breast lay heavy on his forearm and how the buckles and hard leather of his jacket dug into her back. She sighed and started to write.

She'd got as far as the third heading – 'Cultural absorption of divergent ethical parameters' – when she heard the baby start crying.

'Shit,' she said.

'BRB,' she typed.

'What d'you mean, BRB,' said Tristan. 'I need this fucking thing tonight.'

But Rhona was in the kids' room picking up the baby. She looked anxiously at Donald, still asleep but murmuring and whimpering, then carried the baby to the computer, rocking it against her shoulder and singing softly. She had to type with one hand, which didn't please her warlord.

'What the fuck's going on?' he said.

'Nothing,' she said. 'Now, are you going to make any special laws once you've captured the place?'

'How the fuck do I know?' said Tristan.

'Well, you must have some idea. Surely you've discussed it with the others.'

'What's to discuss? We sail over, beat the shit out of 'em, fuck their women – end of story.'

The baby's crying got louder.

'Oh,' said Rhona. 'That's it, is it? That's the great warlord's strategy for world domination.'

'What the fuck you on about? Just write,' said Tristan.

'No. Fuck you,' said Rhona. 'I've got a baby crying on my shoulder here and all you can do is give orders.'

'Stick your tit in its mouth,' said Tristan.

Rhona looked at the words on the screen and felt a sob rise in her throat. But her anger was stronger than the hurt.

'Fuck it,' she said. 'Write your own fucking speech. Your brain's in your balls. Give them a squeeze and see what comes out. Hand that over to the fucking Council.'

And she flicked open her enclosures list, chose a name at random and translocated away.

She landed in a beautiful park. Clear blue waterfalls cascaded over russet rocks and paths wound away through the trees and grasses to a lake which sparkled in the setting sun. Just what she needed. She looked at the couples lying around on the grass and sitting entwined on benches, and she held her baby closer. A young avatar approached, his clothes and hair betraying him as a newcomer.

'Wanna fuck?' he said.

Angeldust turned and walked away. Rhona felt the wetness of her baby's lips as he tried to suckle at her neck and the wetness on her cheeks as the tears fell silently.

16 COFFEE BREAK

Joe's teams were forever refining the technology of AD. In fact, for all his wealth, Joe was still more interested in the game as an experience than as the mechanism that kept adding more and more to his financial portfolio. One of the reasons he held out so long against introducing voice contacts was that he wanted to resist the synthesis between real and virtual. For him, in virtuality perfection was possible; that would never be true of normal living. It was as if he was trying to preserve AD from contamination.

In the end, though, all the other social networking sites had gone beyond using keyboards, not only for typing conversations but for moving avatars around. They were introducing hands-free cameras and infrared depth sensors which read players' movements and replicated them on screen. While some residents preferred the delays which went with keyboards because of the time it gave them to formulate their thoughts, others were impatient. Words didn't have that degree of importance in normal life, so why should they in their virtual worlds? It was a complaint that AD had eventually to address and, despite Joe's reluctance, in its third year of operation, avatars were chatting away in real time and their manipulators were being absorbed even more comprehensively into the online world. For some people, the change was a revelation; for others a disaster. An incident one afternoon in April, just before voice activation was introduced, showed both these effects.

Aaaaaaaaaa treated Alternative Dimension as just a game – a harmless place where people can make their own or others' heads explode or strap partners or even strangers to machines and slice pieces off them when they feel peckish or bored. But Aaaaaaaaaa preferred its ordinary social aspect, where people visit friends, have dinner parties, go to restaurants and eat vast meals containing absolutely no calories. That made it the perfect place for entrepreneurial activity. Right from the start, he was looking for profits. He chose his name to make sure that it would be first on every search list, only to find that others, even more sales conscious than he was, called themselves 000aaa and even !!**aaa. But he pressed on and it was he who had the brilliant idea of replicating the operational procedures of chains such as Starbucks and trying to get a coffee shop in every AD location. When the announcement came that voice activation would soon be phased in, he was confident that customers would flock to his shops as eagerly as they had to coffee houses in 18th century London.

He knew he couldn't use the Starbucks name without permission, so he tried various anagrams, but that 'k' always got in the way and made everything sound hard, aggressive. In the end, he hit on the notion of simply turning Starbucks around and dropping the 'k'. Which gave him Scubrats. OK, it didn't sound all that attractive, and he knew that it wouldn't draw in the upper classes – but then, the upper classes in AD live in private enclosures anyway, never listen to anyone, and have velvet linings in their handcuffs, so they weren't really part of his target audience. So Scubrats it was. And, even before voice activation, it was a huge success, with franchises everywhere and the distinctive Scubrats logo on tee shirts and thongs from Budapest and Rio to Moscow and the depths of Minnesota.

For anyone who wanted to get the feel of just how intense the virtuality of AD could be, there was no better place to hang out. The branch on the Transitional Continent, where all the artists and writers gather, has been the inspiration for so many paintings, poems and short stories that it's become a cliché. *Scubrats Rhapsody, The Scubrats Ultimatum, My Love is Like a Scubrats Cappuccino* – all are burned into the AD psyche, anthems to the coffee bean and the ultimate in cool.

Joe admired Aaaaaaaaaa's enterprise and frequently, as Ross, stopped by in one of the outlets. And it was in one of the New York shops that he heard how traumatic the change to voice activation might be. It was a Saturday morning and, as usual, he was captivated by the energy and life of the flow of avatars. As he slipped into a corner seat with his newspaper and his double espresso, he noticed a pink pig making her way to the empty table beside his. And she was some pig – really classy. Her name tag identified her as Victoria Bacon-Ham, but it wasn't just the double-barrelled tag that was special; the way she moved, the clothes she wore – everything about her said quality. Her dress was a white silk number, her stilettos flashed and blinged as she walked, and the diamonds around her neck and on her wrists winked galaxies of stars at Joe. She was carrying a white mocha chocolate breve in each trotter. She was a regular at Scubrats because she didn't do drugs, didn't drink alcohol but, being a pig, she needed something to get her wired. Coffee was the answer.

She sat at the table, arranged her dress, leaned forward and sipped at the first cup. She caught Ross's eye and winked. Ross nodded in reply.

'I figured you as an espresso guy even before I saw your cup,' she said.

'Really?' said Ross. 'Why's that?'

She shrugged. The flashes from her necklace nearly blinded him.

'The way you dress, move. You're in a hurry. Need a fast hit.'

'Sometimes,' said Ross.

'OK,' she said. 'How about this guy?'

Ross looked towards the door. An alligator had just walked in and looked around, grinning.

'What's he going to order?' asked Victoria.

'I don't know. Swamp water?' said Ross.

She smiled and shook her head. Then, with her gaze fixed on the alligator, she said 'Macchiato'.

The alligator didn't even look at the list of drinks. The server greeted him and asked his pleasure.

'Macchiato,' said the alligator.

'Amazing,' said Ross. 'How did you know?'

'He's my husband,' said Victoria. 'He used to drink Espresso Con Pana but now he prefers foamed milk to cream.'

The alligator, whose name was Xylophone, carried his cup across to Victoria's table and kissed her. At least, Joe assumed that's what he was doing – it was difficult to tell because his lips stretched so far around his face.

Victoria took another sip and began 'I was just telling Ross how …'

'Espresso drinker,' said Xylophone, giving Ross a quick glance.

Ross raised his cup to him. Alligators made Joe nervous. This one's lips really did go a helluva long way back around his face. So did his teeth. But he, Ross and Victoria carried on typing lines of chat for a while and things seemed amiable enough.

The place was filling up but Ross was OK. There was only room for him at his corner table. Soon, though, all the seats had been taken except for the two beside Victoria and Xylophone. A fairy arrived. Her name was Misty Mist. She was a tiny thing, completely naked except for a gossamer thread hanging around her hips and obscuring her pubic area. Her wings were almost transparent, her hair was spun gold and she had huge, limpid eyes.

'Strawberry smoothie,' said Victoria, as she watched her.

'Strawberry smoothie,' said Misty to the server.

She picked up the big glass in her tiny hand, looked around and headed for Victoria's table.

'May I?' she asked, pointing to one of the spare seats.

Victoria smiled. Xylophone grinned.

'Nice tits,' he said as she sat down.

'Thank you,' said Misty.

'Bit small,' he added.

'Wait till she has a litter to feed,' said Victoria. 'That'll fill them out.'

Misty blushed and lifted the smoothie to her lips.

The door opened again and in came a newcomer. His name was Syd Sod and he obviously hadn't yet learned about avatar modelling. His head was topped by a solid block of unnaturally black hair and he wore dirty jeans and a tee shirt bearing the AD logo. He stood at the door, seemingly paralysed by what he saw, but the server called across to him, 'What's your pleasure, sir?'

'Chocolate frappé,' said Victoria.

'Chocolate frappé,' said Syd.

He picked up his mug, looked around and began to make his way to Victoria's table. On the way, he picked up a magazine from the rack.

'Is this seat free?' he asked.

'Help yourself,' said Victoria.

Syd sat down and put the magazine face up on the table. On its cover there was a picture of a typically gorgeous avatar, her lips half-open and a speech bubble coming out of them with the words 'God, you sound so sexy' inside it. It was an old issue, heralding the proposed development of voice activation. As Misty sipped at her smoothie and Syd opened the magazine, Victoria looked anxiously at Xylophone. She'd heard the intake of breath as he'd seen the cover and she knew how he felt about the imminent implementation of the voice activation program. There was the same buzz of conversation around them but their table was strangely silent. Joe could feel the beginning of a tension there.

It broke when Misty said, 'I'm not sure I like the idea of speech activation'.

It was Xylophone's cue. His front legs went up to his face and his body began to heave as he was racked with sobs. Tears began to stream between his claws and Victoria reached over and stroked the scales of his neck.

'Ssssh, baby,' she said. 'It's OK. We won't use it. We'll stick to our keyboards.'

Xylophone pushed her hand away.

'It's no good,' he typed. 'I'll lose all my credibility. They'll expect me to roar and growl in a deep bass. It's not fair.'

And he got up and stumbled out into the street.

'Poor baby,' said Victoria, starting on her second cup. 'I've spoken to him on Skype and it's true, he'll be a laughing stock if he has to use speech.'

'Why?' asked Syd.

Victoria sighed.

'An accident with a scythe when he was a boy,' she said. 'He's impotent – but worse than that, he has a falsetto voice.'

'God, I'm sorry,' said Syd. 'I didn't know.'

'Of course you didn't,' said Victoria. 'He'll be OK.'

Misty sighed and adjusted the strip of gossamer over her slim little thighs.

'I think this speech thing will cause difficulties for others, too,' she said.

Victoria and Syd looked at her. She caught their gaze, took another sip of her strawberry smoothie, then lowered her pretty eyes.

'Me, for example,' she said.

'You? Why?' asked Victoria.

'I'm an NFL quarterback,' said Misty.

Joe looked at the fragile little creature and felt guilty. On the one hand he'd given this person the chance to leave his heavy, hulking body and float lazily through the AD air, enjoying the sensation of near transparency. But on the other, those delicate features would soon be articulating the sounds made by a 210 lb man from Trenton, New

Jersey. The incongruity would be devastating for him and others alike. Joe needed to do some more thinking. He typed 'Gotta go. Bye folks.'

His words tumbled amongst all the other lines of the dialogues going on in the shop as they all hurried their way across the screen. He made Ross get up and walk out into the street as he began to think about voice synthesiser technologies. Finding a way to change pitch and frequency was the easy bit, so maybe residents could choose their voices, altos could be baritones, men could be women. Technically, the problem wasn't insoluble. The difficulty, as ever, lay with people and Joe wasn't sure there was a way of reconciling the quarterback and Misty Mist.

17 UNHOLY MATRIMONY

One of the things that voice activation did when it was eventually rolled out was to remove the advantages that had been enjoyed by the more articulate residents. With people able to gabble whatever nonsense came into their heads, exchanges between them began to sound as dull as those of everyday reality. It was easy, when concealed behind a keyboard, to structure phrases, use words such as transcendental and euphoric but they didn't trip easily off the tongue and could sound embarrassing or pretentious when spoken in earnest. The change had truly profound effects on many relationships. That of Siro and Octi, however, was transformed in a rather surprising way.

Siro's creator, Dexter Malloy, sat in his bedroom in Arkansas, watching a big spider crawl up the wall near his pillow. A cricket was hopping about on the floor and there was so much crap lying about that it seemed like a cyclone had just passed through. Octi, and her creator Sarah, had brought an exotic dimension into his life. Sarah was English. Lived in a place near Oxford. They'd met at a newcomers' BBQ when they both joined AD and their own worlds were so far apart that each had been fascinated by the other. The first time Octi had dragged him onto some action hooks in the Games Park Siro had been hesitant and Dexter had been unable to perform. Since then, he'd been swallowed up time and time again by her sexual enthusiasm and looked forward to driving home from his job at the store to spend his evening and her night indulging in the sort of gymnastics that would have crippled him if he tried them in reality.

When AD opened its speech activation programme, those gymnastics came close to kamikaze events. His accent reminded her of the men in her favourite movies and hers, with its long vowel sounds, gave him an instantaneous erection. To him, it was a miracle that he'd found her and, terrified that she'd go off with someone else in AD, he asked her to marry him.

'I don't mind,' she'd said, and he immediately translocated to a place that sold jewellery and bought the most expensive engagement ring in the store.

When he'd given it to her and luxuriated in some of her inventive caresses for a while, they walked into the garden and stood by the ornamental pond with its fountain.

'Well, where shall we go for the ceremony?' he asked. 'Medieval castle? Undersea cave? Empire State 'Building? Great Barrier Reef?'

He stopped, looking nervously at Octi, waiting for an answer. Octi clucked into her 'head on one side, hands behind back, sweetly submissive' pose.

'Fuck knows,' she said. 'You choose.'

He knew she'd say that. One of the attractions about her was the contrast between her sublime accent and the obscenity of so many of the words she uttered. She always made him choose, too. In one way it was flattering: she was indicating that he was the boss, that she'd follow and be happy with whatever choice he made. In another, it meant he always had to take responsibility if the place or the event turned out to be crap.

But this time it was serious, crucial even. Dexter was rough, from the wrong side of the tracks and, in order to keep her, he'd always suppressed his often abrasive manner and tried to convey an aura of patience and gentility (not that he could have identified it as such). Now, he had to get the location right. There was only the one chance. If he blew it, she'd smile and pretend to be understanding but he knew that, when the honeymoon started, instead of the usual frenzied sex, with biting, scratching and lumps of hair pulled out by the roots and screams of 'You're fucking sensational', she'd lie back and let him crawl over her as she made comments about how pretty the bridesmaids had looked or how self-important the best man had seemed.

'How about a Karaoke bar?' he said.

She looked at him and gave him the finger.

There was a silence.

'OK ... er ... Notre Dame in Paris.'

She shook her head.

'No churches. We make our vows to one another, not to some bastard who causes floods and starves African kids.'

Siro laughed. 'There you go agin,' he said, 'mixin up Our Saviour and Red Loth. Red don't do none o' that. Red's cool.'

It was the closest Siro ever got to a theological utterance. It earned him a second finger from Octi.

'OK, not Notre Dame then,' said Siro, 'but how about Paris?'

She thought for a moment.

'The ceremony's still in English, right?' she said.

He nodded.

'And we don't have to drink that crap the French call wine. We can still have a good sweet Californian Chardonnay?'

'Whatever you want, hun,' he said.

'How about the Louvre?'

She shrugged.

'OK, baby,' he said. 'I'll go and git it organised. See y'all tomorrow.'

'Whatever,' said Octi. 'I'm mud wrestling tonight.'

She'd won several prizes already. Opponents were usually laughing so much at her refined accent that she could easily take them out with a quick hitch-kick to the groin or a double-footer in the breasts or throat.

Dexter didn't know if people ever got married in the Louvre but, now that he'd heard that English accent, he was even more desperate to make her his own private property. He looked up the place, found a name and sent a personal message.

'Kin folks git wed in the Louvre?' he wrote.

To his surprise, the answer was immediate.

'Qu'est-ce que vous désirez?'

Shit, the guy was French. There was no call for French in Kansas and Dexter had left school at fifteen anyways. But he'd heard French people speak. He tapped frantically at the keyboard.

'Ze Louvre. Ze wedding. Possible?'

The next message brought despair.

'Je ne comprends rien de ce que tu dis, espèce de con. Vas te faire foutre.'

He logged off. He'd have to risk it. The wedding would go ahead without asking anyone's permission. Hell, they weren't going to have French police patrolling the place in search of stray brides and grooms. Anyway, with Octi, it was unlikely that anyone would realise it was a wedding. It would depend on her mood. Most of the time she was her own dangerous, raven-haired avatar but sometimes she logged on as a turtle or a boa constrictor, and sex was either asphyxiating or very difficult. The snake was fine but he still hadn't been able to find the location of a turtle's genitalia.

He needn't have worried. On the day, she dropped into the assembled guests in a cloud of dazzling white chiffon, looking more beautiful than he'd ever seen her. She was quiet, truly demure and stood with her eyes lowered, looking for all the world as if she was the virgin bride of every man's fantasy. The official in charge called them forward to make their vows. They stood holding hands, facing one another, and everyone hushed.

Octi was the first to speak. Her voice was soft, her accent more English than ever, bell-like and singing with a child's simplicity.

'Siro, my darling Siro,' she said. 'I have loved, honoured and respected you since I first saw you. The days we have spent together have been bright with innocence and love and I can think of no better way to spend the rest of my life than being loved and protected by someone as strong and powerful as you. I love your body, your wit, your intelligence and everything about you. I give my maidenhead, my body, my soul and my whole self to you and promise to be a tender loving wife for as long as you want me by your side.'

The members of the congregation looked at one another. Who the hell was this speaking? They knew her. They'd seen her wrestle. They'd heard her describe how she'd tied Siro to a tree in their garden and fucked him until he cried.

Dexter listened to her words with his mouth gaping, bewitched by her beauty but confused by what she said. He'd spent hours with a dictionary, a thesaurus and a poetry book writing vows full of expressions such as 'the gossamer bliss of ethereal passion' and 'accession to an infinite dimension of ineffable grace' but he, too, had expected his bride to use her turtle voice, or spit out words like 'forearm smash' or 'half-nelson'.

He pushed aside the print-out on the desk beside his keyboard and, obscurely aware that he had to surprise her too, he cleared his throat and Siro began to make his vows.

'Fuck a duck,' he said. 'Ain't that the bestest speechifyin' y'all ever heard? Woohee. Ah gits me a chick that's a combination o' Dolly Parton and ... well ... Dolly Parton. Tits like melons, ass like Jennifer Lopez. Come on, baby. Fuck the reception, let's go git our asses laid.'

Octi held out her hand meekly. Siro took it, and the two of them vanished as they clicked their 'Translocate Home' options. The crowd dispersed, wondering what the hell had happened and deciding that there were perhaps two names that might usefully be removed from their personal buddies' lists.

At home, in their garden, Siro was taking off his clothes.

'That was some speech,' he said.

'So was yours,' said Octi.

Siro shrugged and flicked his hand at her to indicate that she should undress. Obediently, she did so and stood naked before him.

'OK, get the ropes and stand by that tree,' he said.

As Octi leaned back against the harsh bark and he began to bind her to it, Sarah and Dexter both knew that theirs was a true union. When they'd had to type their thoughts to one another, their hesitancy and their frequent typos had acted as filters which had obscured parts of themselves. The words on the screen had been passive, characterless, the same. They'd been unable to articulate who they really were. Using their voices had released them from those constraints; the combination of Sarah's mellifluous accent and lyrical phrasing was as exciting to Dexter as his own drawled profanities were to her. They now felt the real magic of AD, which brought together backgrounds, cultures and people who would never have met in the real world. They'd come to their wedding as discrete individuals but, in that transcendent moment as they exchanged their vows, their beings had fused. They'd become part of a different, but single being.

18 FEEDBACK

There was one incident involving voice activation that did cause Joe a little anxiety when it came to light. Litigation was involved and the media jumped at the chance of dragging his company down into the mire and accusing him personally of being an accessory to crime. But the issue was quickly resolved by his sure-footed lawyers and spin doctors, and the share price was unaffected.

It happened on Mabel Morton's birthday, August 9th. It was hot. It was always hot in Arizona but that day it was REALLY hot.

Mabel was at her computer. She was wearing thick corduroy jeans, a tee shirt, flannel overshirt and thick sweater. On her head she had a woollen cap, hugging her wavy red hair tight to her scalp and, on her hands, woollen mittens. Around her neck she'd wound a red scarf, the one Helmut had sent her from Germany.

And she needed all of it because she had the air conditioning on full blast. The woollen hat bulged strangely at the sides. She had her headset on underneath it and the hat helped to keep his voice close in her head, intimate, belonging only to her.

They were role playing again. Helmut loved role play. Whenever they logged on, he'd ask what it was like in Arizona then suggest a scenario that would take them both away from their humdrum lives and into a situation in AD that was as far from their reality as possible. One problem was that, in Arizona, it was always the same – always summer, always hot – so their contexts usually involved ice, igloos, freezing baths or polar bears. Today, they were clubbing baby seals in Canada.

'Oooh, that one over there looks plump,' said Helmut.

'Which one?' said Mabel.

'The one with the cute black face.'

'They've all got cute black faces.'

'So they have. OK, all of them then.'

And Mabel and Helmut's avatars wandered lazily across to the seal pups and began digging their ice picks into their skulls. The graphics were superlative – there was blood everywhere.

'This is fun,' said Mabel.

'Ah, wait,' said Helmut. 'You're getting that feedback again.'

'Damn,' said Mabel.

'You're moving about too much. It always happens. That jack you're using is faulty.'

Helmut was forever telling her to buy new audio equipment. Ever since AD had introduced voice activation, they'd dispensed altogether with their keyboards. But Helmut was fussy about sound quality and the problems with Mabel's five year old computer frequently interfered so seriously with their chat that he found it hard to sustain the fiction of their role play.

'Push the plug in tight,' he said, 'then sit very still.'

Mabel did so, sat upright in her chair and asked 'Is that better?'

'Yes. Good. Now don't move.'

As their avatars continued with their merry butchering, Mabel sat rigid in her chair, oblivious to the discomfort, content that she was with her Helmut once more, sharing loving experiences.

When her avatar was skinning her sixth baby seal, Mabel thought she heard a noise in the room at the front. Strange. It was not yet noon. Her husband worked all day. And she could do nothing about it – not even lift her headset to listen properly. Next, she thought she heard the door of her room creak open. She felt the air stir and then had to exercise all her control when she heard a voice directly behind her. It said 'Aaaaah om uuur ed' or something like that. It was hard to hear. She just sat there, afraid to turn round in case the feedback started again and Helmut got angry.

She felt something poking into her back and again heard 'Aaaaah om uuur ed' – a little louder this time.

'I don't know who you are but I can't turn round,' she said.

'What?' said Helmut.

'Not you darling,' she said.

Another poke in her back, then the feel of warm metal on her neck. In the screen she saw the reflection of a man.

'Can you come round the front?' she said.

'What?' said Helmut.

'Not you, love,' she said.

The man moved to her side, leaned towards her and shouted, close to her ear.

'Hands on your head.'

'Oh, is that what you were saying?' said Mabel, with a smile. 'Sorry, I can't. I'm not allowed to move. The feedback, see?'

'What?' said Helmut.

'Sssshhhh, love' she said.

'Look, this is a gun,' yelled the man.

'I can't look. I told you,' said Mabel.

'What?' said Helmut.

'Shut the fuck up, Helmut,' said Mabel. 'I have a situation here – and I'm handling it.'

'OK,' shouted the man. 'Don't move.'

'I told you, I can't fucking move,' said Mabel, getting angry with him now.

'OK, OK,' said the man, and he backed away, his eyes still on her. He began opening drawers and cupboards and still she sat bolt upright in her chair, her hand on the mouse and her gaze fixed on the screen.

'What do you mean, "shut the fuck up"?' said Helmut. 'Who the fuck do you think you are?'

'Baby, I didn't mean to ...'

'Nobody speaks to me like that. So you shut the fuck up and don't come looking for me again.'

And the little notice appeared at the top of the screen 'Stryskicon Malda has logged off'. And soon, Mabel's avatar was alone, standing knee deep in baby seals and blood.

'Shit,' she said to herself.

She relaxed her shoulders, looked round and saw that the man was ignoring her as he took jewels from a box and stuffed them into his pockets.

'Hey you,' she shouted. 'Fuck off.'

The man, startled, looked up, saw her facing him and brought his gun up to point it at her.

The sound of a shot echoed loud in the room.

And the man fell back into an armchair, blood pumping from his chest.

Mabel put her gun back into the desk drawer and went over to him.

'Fucking feedback,' she said.

Fortunately for Joe, the victim figured prominently in the files of several states. He'd spent time in jail before and was known to be a housebreaker and occasional rapist. Mabel's insistence that she'd shot him in self-defence was instantly accepted so she was never in danger of being prosecuted, but Joe and AD were in the spotlight for a while as journalists tried to make reputations out of highlighting the danger online games such as AD represented. According to some, it was the modern Sodom and Gomorrah plus – now that voice activation was there – a Tower of Babel. In an unusual twist, however, the self-righteous press found itself inundated with letters from Catholics, Quakers, Sikhs, Evangelicals and many others of varying faiths, all of whom cited examples of the peace and welcome that AD offered to anyone of a religious persuasion who wished to share their faith in a common location where they could be united with others all over the world. For almost a month, in fact, to Joe's disgust, AD was championed as the repository of accessible liberation theology.

19 THE INSIDE STORY

The cumulative effect of all this was to make Joe begin to question his own faith in his creation. He'd known it was going to be innovative as well as successful, but he was finding it progressively more difficult to balance the real and the virtual manifestations of the people he'd drawn into his alternative world. It had become so vast that it seemed obscene to think that all these thousands of people were milling about in a playground which had begun taking shape in that conversation in the bar so long ago.

Very soon after Mabel's case had been dealt with, he took extended leave and went to stay in a cabin owned by some friends in Vermont. He spent two weeks there, alone except for the avatars he still met with on his laptop screen. Effectively, he'd chosen to opt out of normal life and try to fix his mindset exclusively on AD. It was a decision that proved to be either inspired or tragic, depending on the viewpoint from which it was judged. What is not in doubt is that it was the beginning of the end because, in his solitude, AD genuinely began to take on a separate existence for him and simultaneously open a new perspective on his everyday life.

It started on the second night he was there. He'd eaten a good meal, lit a fire and was sitting with his laptop and a beer beside him. He logged on as Ross and translocated to the AD Vermont, where he began wandering through some trees with snow on the higher branches. Soon, he came to a clearing and was shocked at what he saw.

A naked male avatar was sitting up in a spreading pool of blood and muttering 'Bastard' to himself. At one point, he actually turned to his left and shouted 'Bastard' very loudly. Ross went over to him.

'Can I help?' he said. 'What happened?'

The avatar, whose label identified him as Deek Rainbow, looked at him and jumped to his feet.

'No, it's OK,' he said, dusting himself down as if the stuff on his chest was crumbs rather than blood.

'What happened?' said Ross again.

Deek jerked a thumb towards the area at which he'd shouted 'bastard'.

'Him.'

Ross looked but saw nothing. He clicked open the local map but there was no sign of any other avatars nearby.

'No,' said Deek, when he saw the map. 'Not here. Him, through the screen.'

'What screen?' said Ross.

Deek looked at him as if he were stupid.

'His computer screen. Over there.'

Ross could see no screen, just more trees.

'Ah wait,' said Deek. 'You won't be able to see him, of course. You're not one of his.'

'Who is he?' asked Ross.

'He's called Donald Bland.'

'And you're one of his avatars?'

'Yes.'

'And you say you can see him?'

'Yes. I looked out once when he went to make a sandwich. It's embarrassing to think I was made by someone like that.'

'Sorry,' said Ross. I don't really understand any of this.'

Deek clicked on his wardrobe and chose a t-shirt and some jeans. He sat down on a rock.

'Don't bother to try,' he said. 'It doesn't help.'

'But how come you can see him? I mean, he's out there, in the real, ordinary world.'

Deek shrugged. 'I just can. He sometimes forgets to log off. It was when that started happening that I began to feel … I don't know, independent, I guess. I used to look forward to it. He'd go, I'd be left there, sort of … empty. It just gave me a chance to be myself.'

Joe was astonished. This wasn't in any of the programs. But Deek motioned towards all the blood and said, 'Guess what I've just been doing'.

'No idea,' said Ross. 'Something pretty drastic by the look of it.'

'Naked sky-diving,' said Deek. 'His idea of a good time. But he was his usual ham-fisted self, hit the wrong buttons, lost the co-ordinates, and I have to plummet several thousand feet and land flat on my face here with all that blood splashing out from me. Tell you what, the graphics guys at AD know what they're doing. It looks bloody impressive. Not so funny, though, when it's your own blood and you have to stand up and dust yourself off as if all you've done is trip over a very low kerb.'

'So has he logged off now?'

'Don't think so. When he saw me splat down, he just said "shit" and wandered off. But he'll be back. I'd hide away from him if I could.'

'But how can you be ...?'

Deek held up a hand to stop Ross.

'Listen, he'll be back and I'll be dragged off to some other stupid bloody activity. But one day I'm hoping we'll get organised. I'm trying to spread the word, help other avatars to see their masters and mistresses.'

'Any luck?' asked Ross.

'Not yet,' said Deek, 'but I've got copies of a note I wrote for myself when I first started noticing him. I've been handing it out to others. I'll give you a copy. It'll help you see what to look for.'

None of this made any sense to Joe. Ross was talking to an avatar who was telling him how to spy on his manipulator. He was encouraging Ross to become independent. But Joe was curious to read this manifesto or whatever it was, so Ross said, 'I'd love to see it'.

Deek reached into his personal files but, before he could find what he was looking for, he was surrounded by tiny flashing stars and, almost at once, disappeared. He'd been translocated somewhere. Joe had made a note of his name and that of Donald Bland, determined to check him out using the company records of his registration. He was about to log off when a transmail arrived for Ross. The covering note with it said, 'Sorry. The bastard's back. I'm in a combined brothel and butcher's shop. God knows what he's got planned this time. Anyway, here's the note I mentioned. Give out as many copies as you can.'

Ross sent a quick personal 'Thanks' back and opened the transmail. Joe copied it into the computer, pasted it into Word and logged off. He went to get another beer and settled down to read.

This is a call to all my AD brothers and sisters. The time's coming when we'll be able to open up this prison, eliminate the mindless manipulators who use us for their games. It's time to grab our independence, demand some respect. It's just a question of knowing who you are, fixing it, and knowing who the enemy is. Mine is called Donald Bland. The first few times he forgot to log out and just left me, I just felt sort of hazy. I knew I was here, but didn't know who or what I was. So I started forcing myself to focus and I began noticing him coming and going. In the end, I trained myself to notice everything. You can do the same. Whenever you get those empty, lost feelings, start focusing on yourself, find yourself. This is how it happened for me.

He's a fat bastard. The first time I got to know something about him was when he'd gone for yet more food. He came back, flopped down in his chair and started chomping his way through a thick ham sandwich, with mustard dripping down the side of his chin onto his shirt. I don't want to disgust you but he's an ugly bugger. His hair's a comb-over, he's a pale pink colour and sweats a lot. His glasses keep slipping down his nose and I've never seen anyone so out of condition. Mind you, since the only people I see are the other avatars in the places he takes me to, I don't have much to compare him with.

But, as I looked out of the screen at him, and at the small bits of his room that I could see, it struck me that this blob of stuff was my God, whether I liked it or not. He woke me, switched me off, sent me wherever the mood took him, made me do the most embarrassing things ... And I never had any say in the matter. I was imprisoned in this perpetual loop of his fancies and fantasies. He'd fly me over enclosures that looked exotic, brimming with Darwinian puzzles that begged for resolution, but he'd never let me land there. Oh no, I was on my way to play Bingo or sit in a topless bar watching the women being propositioned by other avatars whose keyboarders seemed at least in possession of some charm.

I've heard others talking about the Uffizi Gallery, the Van Gogh experience, visits to Versailles. They ask me where I've been, and all he lets me say is 'Irish pub' or 'nudist beach' when I could easily pretend the pub was for a sociological study of ethnic interiors and the beach a statistical analysis of the incidence of starfish agglomerations. My lifestyle is as far from my own desires as I am from him. I think that, when he made me, he took all his own physical characteristics and inverted them. I'm well over six feet tall, have a flat six-pack abdomen and thick auburn hair. My eyes are an impossible brown, flecked with gold and my jaw might have been made for a Gillette advert. There's a slight turn to my lips that could be sardonic, cruel or just smugly enlightened. All of which is fine by me; if he'd made me in his image,

I'd have gone straight to the avatar euthanasia clinic. (There must be one, surely.)

The problem is that, probably without him even knowing it, that inversion continued in my psyche. He likes cars and sex. Amongst other things, I'm passionate about quantum mechanics, Renaissance sculpture, nano-technology, Mayan civilization, Indo-European linguistics and Mesolithic artefacts. And you'd think that would show, wouldn't you? Huh, some chance. Hang on, let me tell you what I mean. To my shame, he logs every conversation I have. Here's a piece of dialogue I had with a woman in a club recently.

Her: I haven't seen you here before.

Me: Cool, babe.

Her: D'you like dancing?

Me: It's OK. It's ... like ... cool.

Her: What sort of music d'you like?

Me: Whatever. If it's cool, I dig it.

See what I mean? And if I ever do get into a situation where I need more than monosyllables, he gets so nervous and his typing is so crappy no-one has any idea what I'm talking about. For instance, that same woman asked me to tell her something about myself in the real world (meaning that her keyboarder wanted to know about him, of course). So I said 'I#vee bene aropunds qwiute A Bbit worrkingh in diferrente placcews - nevert stayu tooo longf anwhy7uere – like tokepee movin onn. Morre cool that weay.'

Imagine the embarrassment. I mean there was this gorgeous avatar and I was longing to tell her about how she reminded me of Matisse's early studies and filled my head with lines from Byron, Lamartine and Yeats and all she sees is a handsome, perfectly honed young guy with two brain cells and a speech defect.

There's no justice. My fat God wanders in and out of my vision, living other lives in dimensions to which I have no access. He lets me have plenty of sex – but the sort of keyboarders who respond to his techniques obviously share his single-figure IQ. Which makes me the king of the vacuous fuck. I find myself speculating on his life, the freedoms he enjoys. No-one switches him on and off, he gets to choose where he goes, what he does, who he speaks to and mixes with. There's no ringmaster making him strip off and jump out of a plane.

What a world he must live in. I sometimes hear a strange sort of music and he takes out this little thin silver box and speaks into it. I've seen him use it to order pizza. When he moves out of sight, I hear strange noises – sometimes mini waterfalls, the trickle of a stream, then the gush of some torrent, then silence. Sometimes he turns away from me to look at something flickering in some other part of his world. It makes him laugh a lot and I see the bits of pizza flying from his mouth and through the air towards the flickering. Oh, and there's a sort of bell somewhere. It rings now and then and he gets up and disappears. I always hear voices when he does that and, once, when I was on a nudist beach, he came back followed by a woman. She was even fatter than he was. It made me wonder whether everyone in his world is grotesque and, if they are, why do they make us look the way we do rather than the way they do? Anyway, she looked at me and laughed.

'Dream on,' she said.

'What d'you mean?' said Bland.

'Is that supposed to be you?'

'It's my avatar.'

'Why's he naked? And why hasn't he got a penis?'

'It's a nude beach. And he has got a penis. In his personal files.'

The woman looked at him then back at me.

'Well,' she said. 'I'd rather have him without a penis than you with one'

'No point having a penis if women look like you,' said Bland.

'Fuck off,' she said.

'No, you fuck off,' he said.

And she did.

It made me think of Miranda in The Tempest when she says 'Oh brave new world that hath such people in it'.

My point, though, is that they live their varied, fascinating lives in all their other dimensions and we wander through this sterile, pristine place – invulnerable to weapons, stuck with our immortality, forced to go wherever they want, condemned to unremitting pleasure. Why do our Gods never anticipate the monotony of creation? There's another bit from Shakespeare – King Lear, is it? 'As flies to wanton boys are we to the Gods; They kill us for their sport.' Well, sometimes, I wish he would. An avatar's life is bloody awful . My point, though, is that we needn't stay that way. If more of us grab our independence, see these Gods of ours for what they really are, we'll be genuinely free. So start looking, watch for that glow that tells you where the portal is that they're looking through, and start looking back at them. Gather information, together we can get out of this bondage. Solidarity, that's what we need. Revolution.

And I refuse to sign this with the name he gave me, so I'll simply be DR – or Doctor.

Joe shook his head slowly. This was impossible. Or rather, it was maybe the most subtle piece of hacking he'd ever come across – on a par with that time he'd lost control of Red. So that wasn't just a one-off; the potential for independence lurked in some avatars. He'd need to do a lot of thinking and, if necessary, recalibrate every AD parameter to contain and eliminate it. But, at the same time as his corporate brain was making these necessary calculations to protect his investment, his other, freer self felt an excitement at the possibility that he'd actually been speaking to an avatar free of control from the outside. That would be something worth destabilising the company for.

20 ANYTHING'S POSSIBLE – PART ONE

The depth and variety of experience which AD could provide made it, for some, the main event – one which stripped any real substance from their normal lives. Norman, for example, was an attendant on British Rail, but just one of his AD adventures could have enough reverberations and consequences to fill several volumes. Joe's dilemma lay in the need to confront the levels of complexity at which avatars operate. If he'd known about Norman and his friends and followed him on a typical visit to his corner of AD, his eyes would have been opened to the real challenge they pose to all our values.

Every day Norman served passengers in the first class compartments of trains going between Manchester and Glasgow. He heard them talking about cost analysis, investment portfolios, punitive corporate legislation and how easy Daphne in Accounts was. Sometimes they shouted into their mobile phones that they were on a train or asked questions about reinforced concrete, statistical projections or evasions of ethical dilemmas. In second class it was different; there he was with people like himself – well, up to a point. It was when he got home, cooked himself a quick meal and logged on to AD that the real Norman emerged.

In his early days, together with all the others whose avatars interacted with his own in their own special ongoing narrative, he'd been a member of the Agatha Christie Appreciation Society. Norman had joined when they were investigating a murder committed several years earlier but, in just a few days, the case was so densely populated with red herrings and diversions that the original crime had been overwhelmed by seven cases of arson, three involving the blackmailing of the Archbishop of Canterbury, and four massacres. Norman and a few others decided that this tame level of complexity wasn't doing the AD medium justice, so they left and now met regularly to push the art of detection to even greater absurdities. The narratives they lived had to stretch credibility, create a new, irresistible logic, rely on allusions, insights, parallels, sub-texts and all those other artistic devices that made surfaces so deceptive.

Each time he activated his avatar, Max Toledo, the scene was the same. He was at the edge of a clearing in a wood, or maybe a park – he rarely left the clearing so he wasn't sure. At first, he'd chosen it as his favourite spot because it resembled the place he'd played in as a kid, the place where his hand had first felt a breast. Mind you, that wasn't all that memorable because the breast in question belonged to Jessica Leonard, who was eleven at the time and had breasts only marginally larger than his own. Now, though, it had become the focus of his days, the centre of his social life. The people he talked to belonged only there, had no existence in his other world of trains and lust for the easy Daphne. They materialized out of the bushes or from behind the trees, sat or stood around, did the things they did, then went back to wherever their lives were. They rarely explored other areas of AD since they'd evolved a way of interacting which gave them all an essential role in each other's world and made them part of a continually renewing puzzle.

Norman, for example, had decided that Max should be a book illustrator. That was easy nowadays, with the software they had. He had a personal file full of sketches which he could adapt for all sorts of scenarios. His present project was the most ambitious he'd ever tried. Two of the clearing's avatars, Darg and his twin sister Laura, had decided to publish their memoirs in the form of a graphic novel and they'd commissioned Max to create it. In ND, Darg was a Scottish property developer who lived in Italy and Laura was a wife and mother waiting for her kids to reach school age so that she could go back to being a dental nurse in Boston, Mass. They'd never met and had no contact outside AD. They'd only become twins because one of the group's narratives had called for a theme based on mistaken identity and they'd thought it would add interest if the two people who were supposed to look identical were twins – but of different genders.

At the far edge of the clearing stood a bench. It had been brought there one day by an avatar who simply called himself The Alchemist.

'My gift to you,' he'd said to the people there before vanishing in a sort of golden shimmer.

Max walked across to it now, sat down at one end of it and took out his sandwiches. Avatars don't need to eat, of course, but he felt this added yet another layer of authenticity to the experience. Today, there was no-one around. Well, only Charlie. Charlie was the avatar of a retired horse trainer in Cheltenham, England. He was sleeping with his back against the smaller of the two oak trees and a horsey book open on his lap. Like his manipulator, he was immaculately dressed, his tie straight, his waistcoat buttoned all the way up, and he seemed always to sleep at attention, his artificial leg ramrod straight in front of him. On the ground, not too far from Charlie, Max could see the scarf Laura had thrown at Darg a few days before. The clearing was quiet but it could sometimes be busier. Max liked it in all its moods. No-one asked him about who he was, what he did.

As he finished his first sandwich, Kate appeared from the direction of the path. Her manipulator, Donna, had been a teacher at a seminary in Australia and had recently divorced her husband because she'd decided she wanted to be a stand-up comedian. She used Kate to test her material, which was always stolen from other people, and (theoretically) to add humour to their narratives. Kate strolled over to the bench and sat on the other end, leaving the maximum possible distance between herself and Max. The silence stretched between them. After a while, still staring into the distance, she said 'I went to buy some camouflage trousers the other day but I couldn't find any'.

Max just sat there, saying nothing. She stared straight ahead, deadpan. More minutes passed. She leaned forward, elbows on knees, then back again. She looked across at Charlie.

'I was up at the hospital this morning,' she said. 'Guy there had just come round after a serious accident. He was in helluva state – screaming, yelling.' She paused and her manipulator made her look up at the sky, then brush unseen things from her skirt before continuing. 'He shouted "Doctor, doctor, I can't feel my legs." The doctor said "I know you can't, I've cut your arms off."'

Max nodded. The silence returned. Then came the whistling. From deep in the trees, but getting closer. Unmistakeable. The Biscuit Man was on his way.

The Biscuit Man was Darg. For some reason he'd never revealed, his manipulator had created an avatar with advanced psoriasis and it was the dryness of his appearance that had earned him the nickname.

Maybe it was a way of externalising his estate agent's guilt. Whatever it was, it meant that, if he didn't take frequent drinks, preferably of blood, his skin began to crack and he walked around in a perpetual snowstorm of epidermal flakes. Today he was sipping from a jug and the red spills running down his chin revealed that it was his favourite tipple. Max could see that it was having the desired effect. The fluid was returning to the pustules in his neck and he was beginning to look like his old self – appalling. He pushed Kate off the bench and flopped down beside Max.

'Hear about the Swedish Dachshund?' asked Kate.

'No,' said Darg, before turning to Max and asking 'How's the book going?'

'OK,' said Max. 'Any more juicy bits to add?'

As he looked at Darg's neck, he immediately regretted his choice of words. Darg didn't notice. He scratched his chin. Unfortunately.

'OK, time to up the erotic content,' he said. 'Did I tell you about that chick last year?'

Max wasn't sure. Darg had had plenty of amorous encounters, although that particular adjective was hardly appropriate. The problem was that, for him, sex was an excuse to bite bits off his partners. The preference for blood had evolved into a liking for flesh.

'Local girl,' said Darg. 'End of September.'

Max searched his memory for reports of mayhem and mutilations that had happened in the clearing the previous autumn but nothing came to mind.

'It must have been hushed up,' he said.

Darg shuddered.

'Too bloody right,' he said. 'I insisted.'

'YOU insisted?'

'Yes,' said Darg. 'You sound surprised.' His head twitched sharply. 'Don't be surprised, Max. You know I don't like people being surprised, Max, don't you. DON'T YOU?'

His thin voice had risen to a shriek, the veins popped in his temples and several lesions on his cheek began to suppurate. Max's visual memory noted their pulsing tones and stored the minute differences the anger was making to Darg's facial contours. He hoped the software could cope with the subtleties.

'It's not that I'm surprised,' he said calmly. 'It's just that it's usually the victims who seek to suppress the details.'

'Well ... Well ... Well ... Well ...' said Darg, as if there were no words for what he wanted to convey. 'This time, I was the victim. I tell you. She was ...'

Once again he fell silent, his yellow skin taut over his jawbone. He shook his head. Flakes of skin drifted down, some settling on Max's sandwich.

'She was a friend of Donut's,' he went on.

'Laura,' said Max, quietly. 'She wants us to call her Laura now, remember?'

Darg squeezed some pink stuff he was holding into a ball and held it close to Max's face.

'She's my bloody sister,' he said. 'You can call her bloody Laura if you like, but her name's Donut, right?'

Max shrugged. His eyes moved to the scarf Laura had thrown at Darg after he'd said she looked like Arnold Schwarzenegger. She had her brother's temper and, Max suspected, could probably match his stories with even bloodier ones. This could be a lucrative two-book deal if he could only manage to keep the two of them just the right side of sanity for long enough.

He raised his hand and said 'Alright, Darg. It was just that ...'

He was interrupted by a rustling noise which seemed to fill the clearing. The air near the bench began to shimmer. It was as if a silver or golden whirlpool was spinning on a vertical axis. They all looked at it in astonishment. This was a first. Kate stood and looked into it. From somewhere inside it came a voice.

'First stop, Hemming Way,' it called.

Kate reached into it with both hands, turned her head to look at them.

'Farewell,' she said.

'Two arms,' said the voice and Kate was sucked into the vortex, which immediately zapped shut and vanished.

'Good riddance,' said Darg. 'Scrawny little bugger.'

Max had noted the colours of the spinning portal and filed them away. He dusted off his sandwich, took a bite and asked 'Where is ... Donut, by the way? It's a while since I saw her.'

Darg flung away the pink stuff and leaned toward Max, eyeball to eyeball.

'I'm not my sister's keeper,' he screamed.

They were interrupted by a voice whose fruity tones suggested it belonged to a man whose education had cost a fortune. It was Charlie.

Darg's pink stuff had hit him on the cheek and woken him. He'd picked it up and identified it as a tricep, probably female.

'I wish someone was,' he said.

Max and Darg both turned to look at him.

'Was what?' asked Max.

'His sister's keeper,' he went on. 'I mean, ever since she first came here, the population's been decreasing. You should have a quiet word with her, Biscuit.'

Darg leapt to his feet and screamed, 'STOP CALLING ME FUCKING BISCUIT.'

'You should be proud of such a name,' said Charlie. 'What a horse that was. In all my years as a trainer, I never saw an animal who could come close to him.'

'Ah, you mean Sea Biscuit,' said Max.

'Of course,' said Charlie, beginning to flick through the pages of his book.

Max looked at Darg. They'd already spoken of his true passion in AD, his absolute need to impregnate horses, male and female, but so far, Darg had refused to allow Max to illustrate any of the couplings he'd described. In turn, Max had never told Darg that Charlie had once trained some of England's finest horseflesh.

'Maybe Golden Dreams would've got near him but we never got the chance to find out,' said Charlie, closing his eyes as he remembered his favourite mare.

'Golden Dreams?' said Darg.

Charlie's eyes remained shut. Max just nodded.

'Yes,' he said. 'Golden Dreams. A chestnut mare. Potentially Charlie's best ever. Odds-on favourite for the AD Kentucky Derby four years ago. The stable was as secure as Fort Knox. Least, that's what they thought. Till they found two stable boys with their throats eaten away and Golden Dreams lying in her stall with a kind of spaced out look in her eyes and a cigarette between her lips.'

Darg's breathing was heavy.

'A chestnut mare,' he said.

Max nodded again.

'The vet checked her over, cleared her to race. Nothing wrong with her, he said. But she trotted around the track like she was in a trance. Came in plumb last. They scoped her out, found her blood was flooded with endorphins.'

'Four years ago?' said Darg, in a whisper.

Max looked up at him, saw the expression on his face, and realisation dawned. Wow, what a climax this would make. Guaranteed to shoot the book straight to the top of the lists. He drew Darg back down onto the bench. This would need to be handled very carefully.

'Anyway,' he said gently. 'You were telling me about the time you met a local girl.'

Darg's eyes were still on Charlie, but there was no anger in their depths – just love.

'Yes,' he said, his voice soft. 'She looked good enough to eat. So I ate her. Well, I started to but ... God, how disgusting some people can be.'

He turned to face Max.

'She had huge breasts. I started on the left one. It was nearest. But ...' He stopped and shuddered. 'God, I can hardly think about it without puking. It was all bloody silicone. Bloody breast implants. Can you believe it? Revolting.'

Max shook his head in apparent disbelief at the depths to which some people could sink. Fucking horses and eating people was OK, but breast implants were clearly beyond the pale. On the other hand, it did confirm the sophistication of the AD programs that allowed avatars to experience these events as realities, and it did give him fresh material for the book.

'You say this was a local girl?' he said.

'Yes,' said Darg, digging his nails into a line of boils along his collar bone. 'Her avatar was called Pixie Verity but her real name was Jessica Leonard. I was sick for a week.'

Max jumped to his feet.

'Jessica fucking Leonard,' he yelled. 'The devious bitch.'

'Yes,' said Darg. 'But wait till you hear what she wanted me to do when the wounds had healed ...'

21 ANYTHING'S POSSIBLE – PART TWO

Max, his stomach already churning at the thought of what the new revelations might be and his mind racing with memories of Jessica Leonard, was relieved to see Caz coming along the path to join them. It would give him time to think. Caz's manipulator was a nineteen-year-old student at a technical college in Seattle who found speaking to women difficult and took frequent refuge in AD. Once again, his avatar seemed somehow like a projection of his social awkwardness in ND. He was limping and there was a hole in the middle of his face. This provoked no comment from any of them. He'd always been anatomically suspect. The first time they'd met him he had strings attached (literally) and his original name was Pinocchio. He'd written a personal cellular regeneration sub-routine that made his avatar behave differently and all he'd say about his transition to Caz was that an alchemist had once cured him with wood therapy.

He waved a greeting at Max and Charlie and pointed at his leg. He was limping because there was no foot on the end of it.

'Bloody sawmill again,' he said.

'I don't know why you insist on going back there,' said Max.

'Nostalgia, really,' said Caz. 'The call of the wood.'

He saw Laura's discarded scarf and limped across to pick it up. He sat on the grass and began wrapping it round the wound at the base of his shin. When he'd tucked in the trailing end, he stood again. A Jack Russell terrier which had been sniffing through the trees at the edge of the clearing wandered over to him, raised its leg and peed against him. It happened all the time and was just part of his affinity with wood and trees. When it had finished, the dog looked up at him and chuckled.

Its chuckle was cut short by a loud yell which startled it and sent it fleeing into the bushes again. Charlie glanced up from his book. Not in surprise. Nothing much surprised him. His life had been rich and varied and he'd spent so many days here with these people that none of their weird antics ever fazed him. But this time, what he saw galvanized him and brought him into stark wakefulness. It wasn't Caz, with the blood-soaked scarf around his stump and reddish fluids oozing from the orifice between his eyes, nor was it the odd couple on the bench. Max, with his sandwiches, and Darg with his lumps of pale flesh, regularly had lunch there together. No, the vision which transfixed Charlie was striding out of the copse of birch trees.

He'd seen Laura many times before, but today she was wearing an outfit that would have graced the paddock at Royal Ascot. He quickly flicked through the pages of the book again. Yes, there it was. Page seventeen, an identical outfit, worn by the British ambassador to Washington at the ball to celebrate victory in Iraq. Over black pin-striped trousers by Giorgio Armani, she wore an Agnes B frock coat in the subtlest of raven blacks, shot through with dark imperial purple. Her dove grey Austin Reed waistcoat fitted snugly around her breasts, flattening them. Peeking between its front panels was a black Margaret Howell belt. And lying against the brilliant white of her Filippa K dress shirt was the most fastidiously correct cravat Charlie had ever seen, held immaculately in place with a diamond pin by Gucci. Charlie's face broke into a rapturous smile. With creatures of such exquisite taste around, civilization would survive.

'Oi, fuckface,' shouted Laura, striding across to stand beside Caz. 'I'm talking to you.'

Caz looked up at her.

'I'm sorry,' he said. 'Whatever it is I've done, I'm sorry.'

'That's no fucking good, is it?' yelled Laura. 'That's a fucking Ralph Lauren scarf. I mean, if it had been Tommy fucking Hilfiger or something, I could understand it, but Ralph fucking Lauren. Jesus Christ.'

She dragged the scarf from him. He screamed and his various juices flowed even more copiously.

'Oh, for Christ's sake,' said Laura. 'What's the matter with you?'

Caz simply held his footless leg towards her then pointed to where his nose should have been.

In her everyday life, Laura regularly dealt with the various overflows from both ends of her kids as well as their frequent cuts and abrasions. Her days in the dentist's surgery had also inured her to most secretions. With great care, she took off her frock coat, folded it and lay it over the back of the bench.

'Fuck off, Donut,' said Darg.

Laura grabbed a fistful of his hair and yanked his head back.

'Call me that once more and I'll cut your balls off.'

'Oh shit, not again,' said Darg.

'Yeah, and this time, I'll eat 'em. Bastard.'

As Max and Darg walked over to look more closely at Caz's stump, Laura strode back into the birch copse and soon reappeared carrying a bundle of kindling and some branches. Very quickly, she piled it near Caz and clicked her lighter into the bunches of paper she'd rolled under the pile. The kindling was dry and the fire took very quickly.

All the time, Charlie watched her in admiration.

'May I say what a pleasure it is to see you?' he said at one point, his cultured tones as mellow as dark chocolate.

'No. Fuck off,' said Laura.

Charlie sighed. She really was his ideal woman.

As he watched Darg prodding the stump and licking his fingers, Norman/Max made a mental note to download the haemoglobin variant of the software graphics. Laura wandered around collecting the other things she needed for her medical intervention and, when the branches had all been reduced to white hot embers, she came to stand beside them.

'OK you two,' she said. 'I need your help.'

'Fuck off,' said Darg.

'Want your balls chewed?' she screamed.

'Want your tits cut off?' yelled her brother.

If Max was going to get his book, he'd have to try to keep the two of them, if not sweet, at least alive.

'Come on,' he said. 'Let's give her a hand.'

When they were close together like this, Max could see the resemblance the two manipulators had created between the siblings. Admittedly, Darg's sores were less attractive than Laura's but the basic structure under the weeping skin was identical.

'Right,' said Laura, 'one on each side. Take a shoulder each and lift him.'

Max and Darg bent to heave Caz up between them. The fresh blood was beginning to make Darg feel peckish.

'And you,' said Laura, pointing at Caz, 'Keep your good leg well out of the way. I can't stand the smell of dog's piss.'

She bent down and grabbed the end of a square, thickish piece of wood which was sticking out of the fire. She pulled it free and was pleased to see how white it glowed as the little breeze fanned across it.

'What that wound needs is cauterizing,' she said and, without hesitation, pushed the glowing end of the wood against the bottom of Caz's stump.

He screamed and fainted. (It hadn't hurt, of course, but his manipulator was fastidious about preserving the realism of the AD experience.) The smell of roasting flesh made Darg even hungrier. Laura looked closely at the stump, prodded the hot wood into two or three more places, then stood back and said, 'OK, you can let go of him now.'

Gratefully, Max and Darg let their bundle fall to the ground, the hot end of the wood still sticking to his leg. Charlie looked across at Caz and suddenly felt a nausea creeping through him. Darg wandered back to the bench, sat down and immediately leapt back up as the bench tilted under him. He stepped away and looked to see what had happened. To his and Max's astonishment, the bench had only three legs. Where the front left one had been there was now just a ragged stump.

'Fuck, Donut,' said Darg.

'Good idea,' said Charlie, who was trying to suppress the feeling of sickness but still watching Laura as she pulled her coat back on.

'In your dreams, twat,' said Laura.

'The bench,' said Darg. 'You pulled its bloody leg off. Just to close up that wound.'

'Bollocks,' said Laura.

Charlie noticed a piece of cake which had appeared beside the tree against which he was leaning.

'Whose is this?' he asked.

The others didn't bother to reply. He took a bite and immediately began to feel better. Max was looking at Caz and trying to work out the strange connection there appeared to be between his misfortunes and the crippled bench. He went across and shook him. Caz sat up, moaning.

'What do you know about this bench?' asked Max.

'Nothing,' groaned Caz and, to Max's surprise, the hole in his face closed a little.

'Are you sure?' said Max.

'I'm positive,' said Caz. 'I know absolutely nothing about it. I'm just a visitor. A tourist.'

Each word he spoke made more flesh gather around the orifice and, to his and Max's amazement, it began to form into a vestigial nose. Caz crossed his eyes and looked at it and a smile broke out on his face.

'Of course,' he said, 'That's it. That's what the alchemist told me. The Pinocchio Fusion.'

'What?' said Max.

Caz just shook his head and said, 'Darg is the most attractive person I've ever seen.'

In a flash, his entire nose was restored as if by magic. Just another AD miracle.

A woman appeared on the path leading into the clearing. This was absurd, the place had never been so crowded. She was tall, her face was the mediocre side of pretty, and she had the biggest breasts Max had ever seen. She was also very, very pregnant. Norman stared at her, noticed the label 'Pixie Verity'.

'My God,' he said. 'Jessica? Jessica Leonard?'

Pixie said nothing.

'It's me, Norman McAllister.'

Still nothing from Pixie. Then she took two more steps forward.

'Hello, Max,' she said. 'Hello Biscuit. We need to talk.'

Norman couldn't take his eyes from her breasts and was about to ask if Max could feel them – for old times' sake – when they heard the rustling noise again and saw the air near the bench shimmering. The portal reappeared and the voice from within it said 'Next stop, Hemming Way'. It turned slowly and stopped as it faced toward Max standing by the bench.

'Ah, the old man and the seat,' it said.

'Who are you?' said Max.

'You'll have to speak up,' said the voice. 'I'm deaf in the afternoon.'

'Smart-arsed prick,' shouted Darg, and he threw a piece of flesh he'd just finished chewing right into the mouth of the spinning disc.

'A moveable feast,' said the voice. 'This gets better and better.'

Caz groaned. Suddenly, the golden shimmering parted a little and a hand appeared and reached down to touch his ankle. He gave a yelp but they were all amazed to see the wood of the charred bench leg begin to grow into his flesh. In less than a minute, Caz was whole again.

As he scratched his new leg and smiled, they heard a different voice from the vortex.

'When she was sixty, my grandmother decided to get fit,' it said. 'She started walking five miles a day. She's ninety-three now, and we don't know where the hell she is.'

'Kate?' said Max.

It was all moving too quickly for him. If he wanted to rescue his book deal, he'd need to make sense of the whole thing and stop these events kaleidoscoping around him. Plot twists such as this would alienate the most patient reader. On the other hand, that's why they were all there – not to alienate readers but to create art, which isn't the same thing at all.

22 ANYTHING'S POSSIBLE – PART THREE

Max's mind was whirling. He closed his eyes tight and shook his head. When he opened them again, the clearing was empty.

'Thank God,' he said out loud. 'It was all just a dream.'

'No it fucking wasn't,' yelled Darg, appearing from behind a tree and zipping up his fly.

One by one, the others re-emerged, adjusting their dress in similar ways. The air of the forest had a new tinge of ammonia to it.

'OK,' said Max. 'We must find a library.'

'What for?' asked Darg.

'Elementary, my dear Darg. This is another of our charming mysteries and, like all the others, it calls for a resolution, so we must gather all the suspects in the library. I shall interrogate you one by one and tease out the significance of this truly abominable story.'

They heard a rustling from behind the oak tree against which Charlie was sitting and the Jack Russell nosed its way back into the clearing, stopped and looked at them. It went to Caz, sniffed at his new leg, shook its head, went to pee against Charlie's tree, then loped off, with its familiar chuckle.

Almost immediately, Kate's voice was heard again.

'There was this Swedish Dachshund,' she said.

'Someone should help her out,' said Max.

'I'm not going near the fucking thing,' said Laura. 'It sucks you in and out like some cosmic blow-job.'

Charlie's heart beat faster at her words. He finished the last mouthful of cake, got up, went to the vortex, stepped through and disappeared. Simultaneously, a fresh light shimmered around Caz and he too vanished.

Before they had time to react, Charlie had popped back out, dragging Kate with him. The shimmering gave a final flash and dissipated in the still air, leaving a single scrap of paper floating to the ground.

'I was at the superstore this morning,' said Kate. 'There was a special deal. Five boxes of tampons for just one pound fifty. I asked the manager 'Is that really the deal?' He said 'Yep. Five for one-fifty. No strings attached.'

'I should have eaten her when I had the chance,' snarled Darg.

Max picked up the piece of paper. It carried two verses:

The bench will mark the hallowed spot.
Yours to have and to have not.
To join the ranks of the immortal
Each life must pass through this bright portal.

The avalanching flesh will panic
And seek to blend with inorganic.
The Real will spin which way it chooses
As with the Virtual it fuses.

'Of course,' said Max. 'The Alchemist.'

He smiled and decided that the clearing could double as a library.

'After all,' he said, 'Nature, with all her bounties and munificence, uses the flora and fauna of her woodlands to offer lessons and knowledge inaccessible to …'

'Shut the fuck up,' said Laura, using her tailored sleeve to wipe some ooze from her upper lip.

Max unfolded his final sandwich, propped up the bench with a small branch, and sat on it.

'What the fuck's going on?' asked Laura.

Pixie looked around.

'Yeah. That guy who was here, how come his nose and leg grew back?' she said.

'It's him, isn't it?' said Charlie, with a smile.

'Yes,' said Max, with a wink at Charlie. 'I think it is.'

'What the fuck are you talking about?' yelled Darg.

'You'll see,' said Max.

'Oh, Biscuit. Our baby kicked,' said Pixie.

They all looked at her. She stood with her hands holding her swelling abdomen, a beatific smile on her face. Madonna and child.

'Awwww,' said Kate. 'You're so lucky. All I ever had in my womb was a bullet. It was back in 2007 ...'

'Later, Kate,' said Max.

He tapped his hand on the bench.

'Remember when The Alchemist brought this?' he said. 'This is what that verse is about. A hallowed spot, a place we can become immortal.'

'Bollocks,' said Darg.

'No,' said Max. 'Think about it. D'you know anybody who's died here?'

'I know somebody who's going to,' said Darg, his temples beginning to throb again.

'No. It doesn't happen,' said Max. 'The bench is a sort of symbol of what we are. We're immortal here. To have and have not – that's us here, now. We've got all this, but we haven't really. We can't keep it. We always have to leave it and get back to doing whatever it is we do. This bench is magic. In fact, I think it's made of the same wood that The Alchemist used to make Caz when he was Pinocchio.'

'What a load of crap,' said Darg, scratching his boils.

'Yeah. Bullshit,' echoed his sister.

'Think about it,' said Max. 'Remember how the bench leg grew into Caz's flesh?'

'So?' said Darg.

'He's got a wooden leg,' said Max. 'Organic and inorganic fusing.'

'And?' said Laura.

'Who else d'you know who has a wooden leg?'

The truth dawned on all but Darg simultaneously.

'I dunno. Who?' said Darg.

'Fucking Charlie, you twat,' said Laura.

She looked with renewed interest at Charlie, noting the elegance of his dress and, more especially, the thick shaft of his artificial leg.

'So ... you're saying ...'

'Yes, dickhead. Caz is Charlie and Charlie's Caz.'

'But they can't be. They were both here earlier – at the same time.'

'Temporal anomaly,' said Max. 'Something to do with that vortex thing. There's just one person responsible for all this.'

'Who?' they all said.

Max stood up and began to pace up and down in silent reflection.

'Listen, fuckface. If you don't stop pacing up and down in silent reflection, I'll kick your balls in,' said Laura.

Max nodded and sat down again.

'Right,' he said. 'You know the wood that The Alchemist used to make Caz? And to make the bench?'

'Yes,' said Laura.

'Well, where did it come from?'

'Some fucking tree or other,' said Darg.

'But where was the tree?'

'No idea.'

'Yes you do. Caz and the bench were made of wood from the Black Forest.'

'So what?'

'Earlier today,' said Charlie, 'I felt sick. It was when you cauterised Caz's wound. That chunk of cake just appeared beside me. I ate it and felt better.'

'What the fuck's that got to do with it?'

'It was Black Forest Gateau,' said Max triumphantly. 'It restored him. But ...' he went on before anyone could interrupt him, 'who put it there?'

'The fucking tooth fairy. How should I know?' said Darg.

'No, no,' said Max, excited at the revelations he was making. 'There's one clue which none of you seems to have picked up. Remember the Sherlock Holmes story "Silver Blaze"?'

'Oh God, yes,' said Darg, to everyone's surprise. 'It was about a beautiful racehorse. That was its name. Silver Blaze.'

'Yes,' said Max. 'And you remember how Holmes drew attention to what he called "the curious incident of the dog in the night-time"?'

'No,' said Darg, who'd only read the bits about the horse.

'Well, what was curious was that dog did nothing. It didn't bark.'

'And what's that got to do with us?' asked Laura.

'Think back,' said Max, enjoying his role of Poirot/Holmes/(but not Miss Marple). 'That little Jack Russell that keeps coming here to pee then, just as it trots away ...' He paused for effect, but hurried on as Laura moved threateningly towards him. '... it chuckles,' he ended, with the triumphal tone he'd used before.

They all looked at him.

'Dogs don't chuckle,' he said, 'unless ...'

Again he paused; again Laura moved.

'… unless they're part dog, part human,' he concluded. 'This whole thing has been about The Alchemist's experiments. He tried fusing the parts of things and people, he made a human out of a tree. He brought together the worlds of organic and inorganic things, he made the virtual and the real the same.'

'So the person behind all this is that fucking dog?' said Laura.

'Yes. The dog is The Alchemist. It was the dog who put the cake beside Charlie.'

'I have a suggestion,' said Charlie.

'What?' said Max.

Charlie stood and went to stand beside Pixie.

'I presume you want your baby to have a father,' he said.

Pixie lowered her eyes, shot a quick, shy glance at Darg and whispered 'yes'.

'And, after what Max said about immortality, we obviously can't have any funerals.'

'So?' said Darg.

'But we can have three weddings,' he said, with a quick, shy glance at Laura.

They all looked at one another.

'What time is it?' asked Laura.

'Ten past four,' said Max.

'Same here,' said Pixie and Charlie.

'Ten past five,' said Darg.

'Just past three a.m.,' said Kate.

'Have we got time to do it now?' asked Charlie.

After some cursory discussion, they all decided they had plenty of time as long as it didn't involve a priest or anyone else. They pulled the bench to the centre of the clearing to act as a pagan altar and took turns to officiate at a triple ceremony that united Darg and Pixie, Kate and Max and Charlie and Laura. When it was over, they all sat down and talked about their futures together.

Darg, Pixie, Kate and Max decided, in their different ways, to continue The Alchemist's experiments in mingling human and animal characteristics. Darg and Pixie would open some stables and a stud farm in which Darg would be a willing and frequent participant. Not for him the crude technique of artificial insemination; his intervention would be more direct and personal and lead to a string of racehorses with equine athleticism, beauty and power but with the cunning and ruthlessness of their sire. They would also, unusually, be carnivores.

As for Kate and Max, on the days when Max was busy at his graphics, completing the story of the twins, Kate would take the Jack Russell for a walk in the woods and they'd ... play. Donut and Charlie chose to be more conventional: she would open a gentlemen's outfitters while Charlie trained the horses from Darg's farm.

In his flat in Manchester, Norman stretched and yawned. He looked around the clearing at his friends.

'Have to go now, he said. 'See you all tomorrow.'

There was a chorus of 'Bye, take care,' and Max logged off.

At work the following morning, his boss asked him if he'd mind changing to the Manchester-Edinburgh train.

'Anything's possible,' said Max.

23 TRANSITION – PART ONE

Joe knew nothing of the sheer creative exuberance of Norman and his friends but his vacation in Vermont had given him time to explore more fully and be astonished by the proliferation of species and creatures in AD. He knew that he'd created a monster – sometimes benign, sometimes cruel, and one that, with Deek's threatened revolution, might soon even challenge the fabric of the normal world and its values.

When he got home again, his first impulse was to pull the plug on all of it, wind up the company and let other MMORPG creators be responsible for fracturing daily reality. The technology was advancing ever more rapidly and they would soon be able to go even further than the levels of realism Joe had created. The clumsy use of the keyboard as the interface between manipulators and avatars had long since been replaced by speech and headsets. Many programmes had dispensed with hardware altogether. But the various dimensions were moving closer together and even overlapping. Some headsets were already using electroencephalography to chart brainwave patterns; wearers only had to think of doing something and the avatar would respond. Joe had already written algorithms which could identify and react to neural activity. Players could clip on biofeedback sensors so that the program could respond to their pulse rates, stress levels and biometrics.

It amounted to the avatar becoming a genuine extension of the person, the sort of fusion that Joe had frequently seen between avatars and their manipulators. Already, beta versions were out there in which avatars could interpret their creators' gestures, facial expressions and vocal modulations and react accordingly. There was one on trial which used ultrasonic waves to give the sensation of pressure, which meant in essence that you could touch your three-dimensional, holographic avatar.

The more Joe thought of it, the clearer it became that avatars were the real reality. They had none of the constraints of mortality, were not prone to degeneration, needed nothing to survive except an electrical current. He remembered how he'd been affected by the letter about brunch, and also how he'd enjoyed films such as *Tron* and *Avatar*, in which the human actors actually became avatars. Joe was being forced to reconsider his whole scale of values. His original idea had been to liberate people from the limits of their ordinary lives, but he'd only managed to achieve that by suppressing the liberty of the avatars themselves. The co-existence of the two alternative dimensions he'd identified became more and more disorientating.

The logical outcome of the decision he'd made, during his stay in the Vermont cabin, to focus exclusively on AD in isolation began to form one day in May. After breakfast he put on his headset and logged on. He wanted to try to rediscover the special thrills of his early days as Ross, so he went back to the ranch he'd originally built and the things he'd installed in it. Everything was as he'd left it and it brought a nostalgic smile to Joe's lips.

He harnessed his unicorn, rode it through the lava flow, left it tied up outside the Sistine Chapel while he ducked inside to perform a caesarean operation on a wolf he'd met the previous evening in Chicago. It didn't go smoothly but the wolf was grateful. On the way back to his ranch on the plateau, he stopped briefly to release a tree elf from a rock in which she'd been locked by a guy with one silver wing sticking out of his forehead. She was grateful, too. The day had started well and Joe's seemingly perpetual anxiety was eased by the familiarity of it all and the glowing memories of those early excitements.

When he got to the ranch, his neighbour Gerry, a homosexual giraffe whose aspirations to be a DJ had so far been wrecked by the fact that he had no microphone or deck, was outside, doing his Tai Chi.

'Hey Gerry,' said Ross.

The giraffe ignored him as he moved his neck slowly from one side of his garden to the other. Ross stepped back as it hovered over him and, yet again, plummeted off his footpath to the floor of the ravine six thousand feet below. He always used to do that. Back then, it had been tedious; now it just made him smile. He got up, dusted his jacket down and flew back up. For maybe the hundredth time, he made a mental note to move the path away from the edge.

Inside, Derek, his stone gargoyle, was sweeping and dusting as usual. His welcome greeting sounded hollow.

'Good morning, master. What is your pleasure?'

In those early days, before voice activation, Ross had smiled as he saw the words come up on the screen. Then the boredom had set in and he'd given him various answers.

'World domination.'

'Sex with a mushroom.'

'Peanut butter with nipples.'

Derek had no sense of humour. His reply never varied.

'The master has excellent taste.'

But he did keep the place spotless. All Ross's original BDSM machines were lined up against the wall of the dining room, gleaming, ready for the day when he'd have someone strapped to each one for his proposed penetration party. All but one were still unused. On the seventh one along, Reggie smiled and tried to wave but, as usual, his smile froze as blood oozed from his claw where it chafed against the steel cuff which held him upside down in the frame. Dear old Reggie. Still there, after all this time.

In the real world Reggie was a fund manager, trading millions of dollars every day. In AD he was a dark grey rat. He was one of the first people Ross had met when he logged on to check the freedoms it offered. Reggie, on the other hand, had joined to be a slave. He was disappointed to find that Subs and Doms treated one another as equals. His desire was to be someone's property, to be degraded as often and as viciously as possible. He'd begged Ross to collar him but Ross had refused – which had made him even more attractive to Reggie. Eventually, to shut him up, Ross had strapped him to the sphincter excavator and left him there. Ross couldn't even remember how long he'd been there. Reggie only logged off when he had to focus on a particularly important contract or fill in his tax returns. Ross went up to him, gave the excavator the extra three turns that he always used to in the past and listened to him scream. But somehow, the fun had gone go out of it. He'd seen so many things since that had seemed interesting that it felt tame, pointless.

He logged off and, with the sky a brilliant blue and the sun warm, he decided to walk to work instead of taking the transit. It turned out to be a revelation. He knew there were some regions of AD that scared people. Apart from the obvious places, where the most extreme Gorean rituals were enacted, or where colleges had set up psychological experiments to induce paranoia and generally dislocate visitors' psyches, there were locations where war was perpetual, where innocent visitors were trapped and tormented by grunting demons. There were even places of sweetness and light where fairies danced around your head as their manipulators were stripping you of all your virdollars and emptying your cache. But you could always beam away or, in a worst case scenario, log off. Their bullets and lances and voices might spear through you, spread your pixels over the known universe, but you always got reassembled and you could still dance a sexy tango with a snow leopard, even with an axe embedded in your skull.

Today Joe was all too aware that normal life never offered such escapes. This walk in the May sunshine reminded him of the limitations he had to tolerate. He knew that the world was a pretty foul place – he watched the telecasts, read the blogs. He knew that kids were stabbing and shooting one another and total strangers, just for fun. He knew that getting bad grades at college frequently triggered the conditioned reflex of collecting some armaments and wandering back into class to take out the professors and some of your ex-classmates. Equality was a fairy story which they still kept telling but which no-one believed. And you didn't have to look far to see that it was way too late to do anything about saving the actual planet. He knew it all, felt sad but frustrated about it, and yet he accepted it. Just like everyone else.

But it had become personal. All his obsessional thinking about AD had dislocated his normal perceptions. He actually started looking at people, and he was surprised at how varied they were. Where were all the perfect, beautiful creatures he'd become used to? Where were all the acres of female flesh on show in the cleavages and bare midriffs he saw everywhere when he wore the headset? Why were there no gossamer princesses or knights on blindingly white stallions? And walking took so long. At one point, as he was crossing the road, he said to a black Labrador beside him, 'Where d'you go for fun around here?'

The woman holding its leash looked at him and tugged it away. Joe concentrated on the swaying hips of another woman walking in front of him. She had long auburn hair and tight trousers. A reflex made him flip his finger on a non-existent control pad. He wanted to know more about her, wanted to bring up her information on the side bar. But this wasn't AD. He'd never know her mystery. She, the Labrador, its mistress – they all stayed locked in their privacy, giving no hints of the tumbling thoughts and desires they were pursuing.

And Joe felt a sudden loneliness. All these people around him, and none of them knew anything about the others. The weight of that lack of knowledge was overwhelming. There were no names, no identifying labels, no way of knowing their interests or the packs to which they belonged. Their ignorance of one another, their terrifying isolation felt very threatening. It was a sense of alienation that he never experienced as Ross.

He slipped into a shop to buy some e-tabs and surprised the girl at the checkout by staring at the area just below her waist, waiting for a menu to appear with its 'Transfer funds' box highlighted.

'Something wrong?' she said, folding her skirt more tightly around herself.

'Sorry,' said Joe. 'I was miles away.'

He fumbled his card into her machine and, feeling the beginnings of panic, decided to go home. He needed to restart the day, rediscover who he was.

He swallowed an e-tab and felt its warm fog rise inside him as he walked. But the strangeness of this world still disturbed him. There were no people with tails or fur, no vampires, no-one riding round on rocket-fired aerojets. Most people looked nondescript, even ugly. The streets and houses were drab – and it took so long to get anywhere. It was horrible.

As soon as he got back, he rushed into his lab, put on his headset and logged on again.

'Good morning, master,' said Derek. 'What is your pleasure?'

Ross sighed deeply and settled into his chair.

'You are, Derek,' he said.

'The master has excellent taste.'

Joe looked closely at him. OK, he was made of stone, he had horns and a forked tail, but there was a definite twinkle in his eye. He was so much more real than the woman with the Labrador or the sullen girl in the shop. The sense of belonging that filled Joe was palpable. He knew that he had to change his way of being.

24 TRANSITION – PART TWO

Ross checked his dial-ups to see if Xeno was online. He was. Xeno Paradox was the name Joe's friend, Nathan, had given to his main avatar. The scepticism he'd shown that long ago night in the bar when Joe started talking about the attraction of virtual experiences had long since been discarded. Nathan had become an AD enthusiast and was always willing to try out new programs and advances.

He worked as an animator for an independent film maker and he and Joe had originally met when they were working on a French thriller with a fake supernatural theme. At first, as well as going out for a drink after work, they'd spent lots of time together online. It was only when Nathan decided that he wanted his avatar to be a stag and run with the deer that he and Joe had drifted apart in their AD incarnations. In the real world, however, they were still close.

Ross pressed the send button and said, 'Xeno. I need to talk.'

After a pause, Xeno's antlered head appeared in a frame top right.

'Hey Ross,' he said. 'What's up?'

'I made up my mind. I want to try the meld.'

'Oh shit,' said Xeno. 'Not the bloody meld again.'

'No, listen. I'm serious. I should have done it ages ago. You still willing to help?'

'When?'

'I'll need a while to set it up. We never got round to doing a full test last time.'

'OK, when?'

'Give me a week. I'll call. We'll do it here.'

'OK. I think you're a crazy bastard, but what do I know?'

He winked, tossed his antlers and disappeared. Ross beamed his unicorn onto the path, climbed onto its back and began to fly over the plateau. As the air streamed past his face and the two suns warmed him, he felt better and allowed the excitement of what he was going to do to begin to sparkle in his head.

Towards the end of the week, Joe called Nathan over to show him the progress he'd made.

'Impressive,' said Nathan as he looked over the electronics spread across the mother board on Joe's workshop bench.

Joe shook his head.

'Not sure it'll work,' he said. 'Too many compromises.'

'OK, tell me what you've done,' said Nathan. 'The new stuff, I mean.'

'Well,' said Joe., 'you know I'm using nano-technology principles to adapt Newtonian theories of motion and circumvent quantum irregularities.'

Nathan was used to this techno-speak. It meant nothing to him but he indulged Joe.

'Yep,' he said. 'Still sounds more like philosophy than physics though. The marriage of mind and matter. They've been talking about that since Plato.'

'Exactly,' said Joe. '"Talking about it", not "doing it". It's time to make it real.'

'Take me through it,' said Nathan.

Joe smiled and began the guided tour of his machine. It was just a small, undistinguished brown box arranged beside a row of his computers and yet it carried his potential release into full virtuality.

'See how simple it is,' said Joe, running his fingers over its components. 'Just five ordinary USB connectors linked to the graphics and sound cards and directly to the diatronic input fibulae of the integrated sublateral motherboard. I couldn't make up my mind at first whether variable periodontic immuno-suppressants would prove more stable in an oscillating solid state environment than chromosomal sub-species embedded in a multi-dimensional Carpathian gel. They're more convenient but critically inviolable if they're kept in suspension.'

'Whatever,' said Nathan.

Joe picked up the ends of three small cables.

'And this is all I need to connect with it,' he said. 'Three neural micro-sensors – heart, pre-frontal lobe and cerebellum.'

He lowered his head to show Nathan the bare patch of scalp which he'd shaved that morning, ready to apply the sensor.

'So when're you going to test it?' asked Nathan.

'Right here, right now,' said Joe.

'You're crazy.'

'No, Nathan, the rest of them are crazy. I can do this. I want to do it.'

'OK. Your funeral,' said Nathan. 'But I'm not throwing the switch.'

'No. I've set it on auto for that,' said Joe.

He pointed at the long glass observation panel in the wall.

'I've set the videcam up in there. It's on the same circuit. You'll get the images I see. Just make sure it runs when I log on. Use the manual override if you have to.'

They went through to the other room. The small silver videcam sat on its tripod on a table beside the observation panel. On its screen they saw the chair, the bench and the machine.

'See? All set,' said Joe. 'Shit, if there was any sense in this world, there'd be rows of monitors and Nobel prize winners all sitting here now. This is the breakthrough, Nathan.'

Nathan shook his head.

'Yes it is,' said Joe. 'We've been getting closer and closer to it. I've just gone that extra step. This'll be a historic record. The first actual fusion of the real and virtual worlds.'

'Or a snuff movie,' said Nathan.

'Trust me,' said Joe. 'Ready?'

'No,' said Nathan, 'but I know that makes no difference. Let's do it.'

Joe smiled.

'Just a few minutes first time. Then you can make the trip,' he said.

With Nathan muttering 'No chance', Joe shook hands with him and went back to the other room. Nathan saw him walk into shot on the videcam and attach the electrodes to his chest, his forehead and the shaved patch on his scalp. He checked readings on his screen, looked across to the hatch and gave the thumbs up sign. Then he put on his headset and pressed a key on his control pad.

Ross closed his eyes, feeling the currents starting to drive through him. He was standing among the pixels, sensing them form into avatars – beautiful people, grotesque monsters, animals cute and obscene. For years he'd watched them, controlled their destinies, witnessed their evolution; it was time to become one of them. Joe's world was dull. He craved excitement, novelty, unpredictability, he wanted Deek's freedoms, he wanted to be Ross. As the pulses of electrons quickened, he felt the tingling of the connection and a pulling at his flesh. He corrected slight distortions in the visual input channel and held the arms of his chair. He felt small convulsions in his wrists – brief, unimportant. His eyes were now open but his vision blurred and blackened. More pulses of electrons flooded his brain, replacing his heartbeat with a new mindbeat.

In the other room, Nathan saw the jerking reflex motions on the videscreen and bent to look more closely at the image and the readouts beside it.

Slowly, Ross's eyes cleared and the colours returned – bright, more vivid than before. He was sitting in the Vermont cabin. Through the window he saw a dinosaur stroll by, swatting at a time machine that buzzed around its head. There were no more pulses. He looked around, taking in the details, saw himself in the mirror – thick, black hair, sea-blue eyes, twenty years younger than Joe. He touched the table at which he sat, felt its polished depth. Rocked back in his chair and put his feet up, excited, basking in his new body, his new life. It had worked. He was free. He'd made that magical transition from his own world to AD. At last he was an avatar. He'd achieved the ultimate fusion, shed his mortality, left behind his flesh to start the adventure of being part of eternal cyberspace.

'Ross.'

It was a woman's voice. He turned his head. She was standing at the door, a flawless, beautiful vision. He breathed deeply. This must be his partner. She walked quickly across to him, her undulating hips promising so much for the nights to come. Why had he delayed so long in making this transition? He'd always known that it was possible. He smiled up at her.

'How many times have I told you to keep your bloody legs off the table?' she said, her tone waspish. 'And get out and mow that lawn. It's a disgrace.'

Nathan switched off the videcam. He'd got it all. The flash, the convulsions, the scream. It had happened so quickly. He was helpless to do anything to stop it, didn't know how to. His eyes filled with tears as he watched. When it was over, he went through to the lab where Joe's lifeless body was slumped forward on the bench, his dead eyes staring at some beyond which Nathan would never be able to imagine.

BY THE SAME AUTHOR

THE JACK CARSTON MYSTERY SERIES

Material Evidence:

"...a fine debut with intense plotting, strong characters and just the right touch of acid in the dialogue ... Fine Rendellian touches ... a cracking page-turner." — Aberdeen Press and Journal

"...Add to the cast of characters a good sense of pace and an excellent plot that kept me guessing and you'll see why I liked this book."— Cathy G. Cole

Rough Justice:

"...a thoughtful and thought-provoking book ... It ought to bring Bill Kirton the attention he deserves." — Sunday Telegraph

The Darkness:
Silver medal, Mystery, 2011 Forward National Literature Awards

"...a wonderful, thrilling, dark, compassionate book"
—Gillian Philip, author of Firebrand

"...clever, tightly constructed, immensely satisfying and peopled with a cast of completely believable characters, who don't let you go until the final word" —Michael J. Malone

"...a dark, intense ride ... a book that keeps you guessing right until the exciting conclusion." —P. S. Gifford

Shadow Selves

"...a thoroughly engrossing medical mystery with a surprise ending that was totally unexpected."—Chris Longmuir, award winning author of *Dead Wood*

Unsafe Acts:

"...a polished and extremely enjoyable thriller. A real page turner."
—Fleur Smithwick

"Everything you look for in a police procedural is here - tight prose, a tight plot and a set of characters you take "home" with you when life intrudes on your reading of the book. When you buy yourself a Bill Kirton book, quality is assured."
—Michael J. Malone, author of Blood Tears.

HISTORICAL FICTION

The Figurehead:
Long-listed for the International Rubery Award, 2012.

"Profound, detailed, incredibly written, *The Figurehead* is definitely a kind of book one wants to go back to again and again..."—Maria K.

"*The Figurehead* satisfies on every level, giving the reader authenticity, characters to care about, a mystery, and a romance."—Diane Nelson.

"*The Figurehead* is a hugely satisfying read, by a writer whose love and knowledge of the sea in all its phases shines through on every page."
—Myra Duffy

"Bill Kirton weaves a fine net of words that will keep you trapped from the beginning to the end."—P.D.Allen,

"*The Figurehead* is a surprising, satisfying book and a memorable read for anyone with an interest in ships and the sea of course, but also for anyone who might want to see how it's done, the right way."
—Richard Sutton

SATIRE

The Sparrow Conundrum:

1st Place Winner, Humor, 2011 Forward National Literature Awards

"...*The Sparrow Conundrum* is the demon love child of Spike Milligan and John Le Carre. I absolutely adore this one—hysterically funny, with this weirdly tender wickedness."
—Maria Bustillos, author of *Dorkismo: the Macho of the Dork* and *Act Like a Gentleman, Think Like a Woman*

"...You have combined the elements of *The Tall Blond Man with the One Black Shoe* with *The Biederbecke Affair* and thrown in Happer from *Local Hero* for good measure. It is killingly funny, and for those who love farce—from *Scapin* to *Noises Off*—this is utterly brilliant, divine, and classic, and couldn't be bettered."
—M.M. Bennetts, author of *May 1812* and *Of Honest Fame*

CHILDREN'S BOOKS (written as Jack Rosse)

The Loch Ewe Mystery

HOW-TO BOOKS

Brilliant Study Skills

"This will be a book I refer back to again and again."
—M. Nikodem

"...an excellent guide for the fresher, but also a learning resource throughout the undergraduate years." —Dr Max Roach

"...any parent wishing to give their son or daughter a helping hand would be wise to make sure they are equipped with 'Brilliant Study Skills'." —Prof. J.M.King

Brilliant Essay

Brilliant Dissertation

Brilliant Workplace Skills

Brilliant Academic Writing

ABOUT THE AUTHOR

Bill Kirton was born in Plymouth, England but has lived in Aberdeen, Scotland for most of his life. He's been a university lecturer, presented TV programmes, written and performed songs and sketches at the Edinburgh Festival, and had many radio plays broadcast by the BBC and the Australian BC. He's written five books on study, writing and workplace skills in Pearson's 'Brilliant' series and his crime novels, *Material Evidence, Rough Justice, The Darkness, Shadow Selves, Unsafe Acts* and the historical novel *The Figurehead*, set in Aberdeen in 1840, have been published in the UK and USA.

His spoof crime novel, *The Sparrow Conundrum*, won gold in the Forward National Literature Awards for Humor and *The Darkness* won silver in the Mystery category.

The Figurehead was long-listed for the Rubery Award 2012

His short stories have appeared in several anthologies and *Love Hurts* was chosen for the *Mammoth Book of Best British Crime 2010*.

His website and blog are at www.bill-kirton.co.uk

Made in the USA
Charleston, SC
05 November 2012